LIKE A DUCK

Deborah Kerbel

Scholastic Canada Ltd.
Toronto New York London Auckland Sydney
Mexico City New Delhi Hong Kong Buenos Aires

Scholastic Canada Ltd.
604 King Street West, Toronto, Ontario M5V 1E1, Canada

Scholastic Inc.
557 Broadway, New York, NY 10012, USA

Scholastic Australia Pty Limited
PO Box 579, Gosford, NSW 2250, Australia

Scholastic New Zealand Limited
Private Bag 94407, Botany, Manukau 2163, New Zealand

Scholastic Children's Books
Euston House, 24 Eversholt Street, London NW1 1DB, UK

www.scholastic.ca

ONTARIO ARTS COUNCIL
CONSEIL DES ARTS DE L'ONTARIO
an Ontario government agency
un organisme du gouvernement de l'Ontario

Library and Archives Canada Cataloguing in Publication

Title: Like a duck / Deborah Kerbel.
Names: Kerbel, Deborah, author.
Identifiers: Canadiana (print) 20200282204 | Canadiana (ebook) 20200282212 |
ISBN 9781443175760
(softcover) | ISBN 9781443175777 (ebook)
Classification: LCC PS8621.E75 L55 2021 | DDC jC813/.6—dc23

Photos ©: Collage_Best/Getty Images; Shutterstock.com

6 5 4 3 2 1   Printed in Canada 114   21 22 23 24 25

MIX
Paper from
responsible sources
FSC® C016245

For my Dahlia

Dear Papa,

My birthday's tomorrow.

One more sleep and I'll officially be old enough to . . .

1- babysit

2- legally ride in the front seat

3- swim unsupervised at the community centre pool

Which means I'll be technically practically almost an adult.

Do you ever think of me on August 27th?

Or is it just another regular day in summer?

Is it even summer where you are?

Your daughter,

Sarah

How It Started

The first crack in my busted-up summer showed up on the night of my twelfth birthday. Inevitably. Because no matter how much you might think you deserve just one single, perfect, cake-filled, problem-free day a year, something bad always has to come along and mess it up. Amirite?

I was scraping up the last smudges of icing from my plate when Mombo broke the news.

"That's a joke, right?" I said, pausing with my fork in mid-air. I glanced quickly at Webster to see if he knew anything about this. But his raspberry-stained face seemed just as surprised as mine.

"I know you're disappointed," my mother replied, her thin eyebrows doing that twitchy, jerky thing they do when she gets upset. "But we'll still have our evenings together. And it's just for one short week." Her words came out slow and steady — kind of like how you'd talk to a growling dog. Definitely not a funny-ha-ha kind of voice.

Which meant this was for real.

My fork dropped to my plate with a clatter. Mombo flinched. These were her best dishes — dug out from the depths of the china cupboard just for special occasions.

"But this is my birthday week," I said. "Our *one* 'You and Me' week of the year. You know that." The last week of summer has always been reserved for the Lasagna girls. Mombo books holiday time off work and it's movies, manicures, breakfast in bed, take-away dinners, and monster marshmallow smoothies for seven whole days. We've never had money for a proper vacation, so we've been doing this ever since I can remember. And it's always just the two of us and sometimes Gran joins us for a movie or two (even though she's a Cameron, not a Lasagna). And Webster is included, of course. He's the only male allowed.

"I know, I know . . ." Mombo replied, putting down her teacup with a sigh. "But Helen fell and broke her ankle this morning, and Doug and Shayna are off on vacation — not together of course — and Jill really needs me to cover for her—"

"I won't go to French cooking camp!" I crossed my arms tightly in front of me.

"—and there's nobody else to ask because we've been short-staffed after our last intern quit in June . . ."

"Not. Happening."

". . . and it's not like this was my choice . . ."

I shook my head so hard my neck hurt. "Uh-unh."

"But, darling . . ."

"Don't even try to make me!"

"Oh, crumb," Mombo said, slumping in her chair and letting out a long sigh. She looked like a tiny blond balloon slowly leaking air. Unfortunately, my heart was too busy imploding to sympathize.

I should have known something terrible was going to spoil this day. Because it had been going so great up until this point — I guess too great. This morning I'd somehow managed to convince Mombo to let me get neon green elastics on my braces at my next orthodontist appointment, even though she said they would look "vulgar" and everyone will probably think I have lettuce stuck in my teeth. And then this afternoon, she drove us down the coast to an actual beach so Webster and I could go body surfing, and the ocean was warm and the sun was shining and the waves were just the right height. And then tonight before dinner, I finally got the phone I've been begging for all year. I didn't even care that it was Mombo's hand-me-down, and that she got the shiny, straight-from-the-box new one. All I cared about was that it worked. And that I had my own number and enough memory to download the FindYourPeeps app I'd seen advertised on the back page of the travel section of Grandad's newspaper. It had been a perfect day up until this moment. And now, with my birthday candle smoke still fresh in the air, she decides to drop this cooking camp bomb on my head?

I could feel tears starting to pile up in my eyes. Losing something you love stings. Mombo knew this just as well as I did.

"I . . . I don't even speak French!"

She laughed wearily and lifted her hair off her neck. Two delicate trickles of sweat ran down the sides of her face. "Don't be silly," she said, fanning herself with her spare hand. Two days ago, the A/C in our apartment broke down for the third time this summer. It was literally like a sauna in there. And I'm not saying *literally* just to be dramatic. I mean, if Webster was capable of perspiring, he'd probably be dripping right along with us. "You don't have to speak it. Just cook the recipes."

Please, let this be a nightmare. "I. Don't. Cook. You *know* that!"

"Well then, this would be a perfect time to learn, wouldn't it? You're twelve now, darling. Not a baby anymore."

"Then why are you treating me like one?" I shoved

my plate away so hard, it flew across the wooden table and very nearly dropped off the other side. Webster let out a squeak and shrunk back in his seat, his dark eyes round with concern.

I shot up, pushing my chair back with a floor-ripping screech. "You don't understand," I said, struggling so hard to keep my voice from breaking. I knew if I cried, it would be game over. I had to stay strong if I wanted to hold on to any chance of changing her mind. "I want to spend the last week of summer with *you*. Like we *always* do. Not rolling dough in a stupid kitchen with a bunch of pre-teens sharing sob stories about our life-ruining parents."

Mombo straightened back up slowly and let out a sigh. "I'm sorry, darling, but you don't have much of a choice."

"Webster and I could stay with—"

"I already asked," she said, standing up to clear the table. As usual, her lace-trimmed apron had not a wrinkle, stain or crumb on it. And as usual, my T-shirt had all of the above. "Gran says she's sorry but she can't have you there. Grandad will be recovering from his hernia operation and needs peace and quiet."

Was it my imagination or was she clattering the dishes a little louder than normal?

"We could be quiet."

"She said it's doctor's orders."

"So, let us come with you to work."

"That's an option, but you'd have to come alone. You know how Jill feels about having Webster in the shop."

Jill is the owner of the gourmet catering business Mombo manages. She has strict rules about hygiene.

I slumped against the wall, searching my brain for a way out of this mess. Normally, I would ask to stay at London Bruin's, two floors below. London is in my grade at school. She has four sisters, and their apartment is so crowded and loud, her parents never seem to notice (or care) when I come to visit. Plus London is super nice to Webster, which makes her okay in my book. But the Bruin family was leaving on holidays to PEI tomorrow morning at the crack of dawn. I really wish there was room in their van for two more! But I'm not that lucky. I never am.

"Couldn't it at least be an *interesting* camp? What about arts and crafts? Or lacrosse? Or . . . anything else?"

Mombo ripped off a sheet of aluminum foil and scrunched it down around the leftover cake. "Believe me, I checked everything else."

"What about that gymnastics camp I went to last

month? I liked it there. I think I know some kids who might be going back . . ."

"I'm sorry, Sarah. I tried. But this was the only camp with any space available at such short notice."

"I bet."

"Come on," she said, rinsing out my favourite I♡NY mug. "They said you could bring Webster. It'll be fun."

"No, it *won't*." I closed my eyes to keep the tears from showing, all too aware that I was on the verge of losing this battle. "Anyway, I'm twelve now. Isn't that old enough to stay home on my own?"

"For short lengths of time, yes. But not all day for a full week. Especially when we're without a working air conditioner. It would be utterly irresponsible."

"Ugh *hic* why do you have to *hic* be so overprotective?"

Great. Stress hiccups. I seem to come down with a honking case of them whenever I get upset. It's like my body's own ridiculous allergic reaction to anxiety. I opened my eyes and noticed Webster was watching me closely.

"Because I love you."

"You don't understand . . . You're *hic*—"

"Ruining your life. I know." Mombo placed the dishes in the sink and turned around, hands on her hips and dimpled chin tilted defiantly in the air. "Forgive me if I don't like the idea of leaving my only child alone all day in a two-bedroom oven."

"But I wouldn't be alone," I said, nodding my head toward Webster, still patiently sitting in the chair beside mine, propped up on a thick pillow so he could see me. My memories from that time are fuzzy, but I'm pretty sure it was the chair Papa used to sit in. *None of this would be happening if he was still around,* I thought grimly.

"Yes, of course you have Webster, darling. You know I love him with all my heart. But let's be honest, he's not exactly a reliable caregiver."

Well, that was uncalled for. Webster let out a sigh and hopped down from the table. I marched over and gathered him into my arms, quickly covering the spots where I was pretty sure his ears were located. "How can you *hic* say that?" I hissed. "You know how sensitive he is."

A hint of a smile tugged at her lips. "But darling, he's, you know . . . a duck."

"So?"

"So? Really? I can't believe we're actually having this conversation. Ducks can't watch over children. I mean, what if there was an emergency?"

"Okay *hic*, maybe he wouldn't be much help in a

fire. Or if a burglar was making off with our TV. But Webster's the one you *hic* want with me in case of a flood. He's the best swimmer I know."

Webster, having successfully wriggled his ears free from my hands, quacked softly at the sound of his name. He craned his neck and nuzzled his beak into my throat — his way of giving kisses when he knew I was upset. Webster has always had extrasensory perception when it comes to human emotions. Somehow, he seems to know exactly when I (and even Mombo) need him the most. Don't ask me how, but he *always* knows. I pressed my cheek to his and wiped the bits of raspberry juice from his beak.

My mother came over and put a hand on my shoulder. Even though I was only twelve, I was already taller than her by several inches. Which isn't as strange as it probably sounds because she's pretty short for a grownup. Gran's short too. "You must get it from your father's side," she told me back when I was eight and we had to start buying my sneakers from the adult section of the shoe store. I don't know if it was on purpose, but she managed to make *your father's side* sound like a bad thing.

"We live on the fourth floor," Mombo pointed out. "I'm not worried about a flood."

"Okay. Then what exactly are you *hic* worried about?"

Her lips smashed together into a thin pink line and I got the distinct feeling she was struggling to hold something back. Webster stretched his neck down and nibbled sweetly on her earlobe while we waited for her to answer. A few seconds of heavy silence wedged between us before she pointed to the clock above the stove and said, in a voice so quiet I had to strain to make out the words, "Time for bed."

Which everyone knows is international mother-code for: *This conversation is over.*

Seven Things You Should Know about Webster

1. He's lived with us since I was two and a half.

Which was the year our family broke. And also the year I forgot how to talk . . . or decided I didn't want to anymore. I couldn't tell you exactly which one because I don't really remember a lot from back then. Most of what I do know comes from bits and pieces Mombo's told me over the years. She remembers it must have been around Easter, because that's when all the new spring babies were born and she'd seen an adorable commercial for chocolate eggs featuring a cute baby duck. A few days before, our family doctor told her that a pet might be "therapeutic" to encourage me to speak again. I can't say for sure but I'm guessing our doctor was probably suggesting a dog or a cat or even a guinea pig. But Mombo had made up her mind about getting me a duck. So the two of us drove over to the Spring Hill Farm and picked him out of a wriggling box full of peeping, tumbling yellow fuzzballs. He was five days old and so tiny I could hold him in one hand. For the next few weeks, he had to sleep in my room in a special crate with a heat lamp and eat from our hands. He was just a baby back in those days, and the vet said we wouldn't know if he was a boy or a girl for a while

— so we decided to give him a name that would work for both. I think we chose a pretty good one.

2. *He's emotionally supportive.*

As it turned out, our doctor was right about the therapeutic thing. Apparently I began finding my words again within a few weeks of adopting Webster. Just a word or two to him at first, but then eventually to Mombo and then Grandad and then everyone else who'd listen. Because he was so great at speech therapy, Mombo got him registered as an official emotional support animal so our landlord couldn't kick him out of the building. I guess she worried I might stop talking again if he wasn't around. I don't know. Maybe I would. But we've never been apart long enough to test that theory out.

3. *People stare at us. All. The. Time.*

It's true. Although I really don't understand why people think it's strange to have a duck for a pet. I mean, how is it any more normal to have a fish? Or a ferret? Or one of those Furby things? Love is love is love. Amirite?

4. He wears a special duck diaper.

Ducks poop a lot. And they can't be house-trained. So unless you live in a barn, diapers are the only way to go. We order special duck-sized ones in bulk off the internet.

5. He thinks I'm his mother.

This is not an exaggeration. It's because of a natural duck instinct called *imprinting* and it's pretty cool. And I guess in a weird way, I kind of *am* his mother. I mean, he wears a diaper, sleeps in my room, and has gone everywhere with me since he was a newborn duckling. He probably doesn't even remember much about his life on the farm, so technically I would be the closest thing to a mother he's ever known. I think that over the years, people in the Spot have gotten used to seeing Webster tag along wherever I go. Everyone loves him. Well, almost everyone. The ones who stubbornly remain *not* on Team Webster are Mombo's boss, Jill, and Ms. Petri, the old lady who lives in the apartment beside ours. I don't know why, but they've got these wild theories that ducks belong in ponds. Personally, I believe both their stone-cold hearts would benefit from the love of a pet. Even something smelly and cold like a turtle.

6. He has lots of nicknames.

Websie-Woo
Feather Butt
Quackalicious
Bird-Foo
Prince Weblington
Waddle-Bunny
Duck-Duck
Donald D.
Daffy McDuckface
and Beaker

7. He's my best friend.

Webster is the world's most supremely fantastic listener. And he's fiercely loyal. And smart and funny. And adorable. And softer and more cuddly than any doll or toy. He's the best pet ever. As long as you live walking distance to a large body of water. And don't mind finding the odd feather in your food. And can handle the quacking.

Dear Papa,

I downloaded a free language app on my brand-new-used phone. Webster and I are learning Italian together! Well, I'm learning it. Webster's just listening to me practise. But only when Mombo's in the shower or sleeping or away at work. She doesn't like hearing Italian. Things that remind her of you make her sad.

Possibly, likely, unfortunately including me.

At least it feels that way sometimes . . .

So, I'm officially twelve now.

If you ever come back, you'll have someone to speak Italian with.

Do you ever think about coming back?

Arrivederci,
Sarah

The Spot

"So, are you excited to get cooking?"

"Hardly," I grumbled, staring out the window.

We were on our way to the BBTS Community Centre. BBTS is an acronym for Blackhead by the Sea — our town's official name. Yeah, I know. *So* gross. The old dude who founded it all those centuries ago must have thought it would be a funny joke to play on all the dermatologically challenged future young residents. Thankfully, nobody who lives here uses the official name. We just call it the Spot. Which is still not great, but anything's better than Blackhead by the Sea.

Our town is tiny. Like, good-luck-finding-it-on-a-map category of microscopic. Like, we-don't-even-have-a-shopping-mall rinky-dink. I don't know what the last official count was, but you could probably fit our entire population inside a small, non-professional-league football stadium. With room to stretch your legs. Except for a few notable exceptions (#ahem #mymotherand-grandparents) most people who live in the Spot were born here. Me included.

The only time I'd ever been anywhere else was when I was five years old and Mombo drove us three hours inland for her childhood best friend's wedding, where I got to be the flower girl and Webster was the ring bearer and we got to wear matching pink bow ties. But we took a wrong turn on our drive and ended up being late to the church and in all the fuss we somehow forgot to put a diaper on Webster and he ended up pooping all the way down the aisle. Luckily, someone pointed it out to the bride in time. But still, she had to lift her big pouffy white dress up to her knees so she wouldn't drag it through the mess. So sad and yet so stinking funny.

Seriously, though — I'm excited for the day I'm old enough to leave the Spot and travel the world. The only thing holding me back right now is lack of funds. And also the fact that Mombo refuses to get me a passport, no matter how much I beg.

Last night when I blew out my candles, I cheated and made two wishes. The first was the same one about Papa I've made every year for the past ten birthdays. The second was for me to travel somewhere on an airplane before my next birthday. Not sure if doubling up on your birthday candle wishes is even allowed. But since there's not exactly a rule book for it, I decided to try. Only it got me worrying while I was falling asleep last night. Do cheat-wishes ever get granted? What if it cancels out my first wish?

Ugh.

We turned into the parking lot and Mombo stopped the car.

"Want me to walk you in?"

"No, thanks," I said, smoothing my hand over the tiny, soft feathers on Webster's neck.

He'd insisted on riding up front on my lap on my first day. As always, he knew when I needed extra comfort. The only reason I'd finally agreed to go to this camp was because Mombo said she asked permission for me to bring Webster. Luckily, the community centre co-director was her second-cousin Jerry — a true-blue Webster fan.

"I don't mind popping in for a quick hello," Mombo said, reaching for the car keys. "It's still a few minutes before the shop opens. I'd love to meet the instructor."

I grabbed her hand. "I'm begging you. Don't make me do this."

She sat back in her seat. "Come on. It's good to get out of your comfort zone. And hey, isn't there a teeny-tiny chance that you'll actually like it? Apparently they've brought in some fancy French chef from Paris. *Ooh la la, soup du jour, déjà vu* . . . right?" Her blue eyes were so wide with hope and I could feel how badly she wanted me to say *yes* so she could drive off to work with a free conscience. But I couldn't do it. She needed the truth. If I had to suffer, so did she.

"There's not even a microgram of a nanometre of a chance I'll survive this day without dying of boredom. And that's assuming I don't throw myself onto the sharp edge of a cheese grater before lunch."

Her eyes widened. And then, to my surprise, she tilted back her head and let out a long belly laugh. Mombo's laugh was like sunshine on a dreary November day. Despite my grumptastic mood, I broke down and found myself smiling. It took her a few seconds to catch her breath.

"Honestly, Sarah. How are we supposed to have any kind of normal conversation when you insist on being such a drama queen?"

"I think the term *tragedy* queen would be more accurate in this particular scenario," I mumbled. Mombo sighed and reached out to tuck a stray curl behind my ear. Her skin smelled like English Rose hand cream and her neatly plucked eyebrows were twitching again. I was still mad. But I didn't shrink away.

"I know you're upset with me."

Webster grunted softly and leaned his head on my

shoulder. I hugged him with one hand and flicked at the lid on the giant thermos perched in the centre cupholder with the other. It was filled with enough Earl Grey tea to last a week for a normal person. And my mother until at least lunchtime.

"And I really am sorry about messing up our special week."

"Me too," I whispered.

"I'll find a way to make it up to you. Promise."

I swung back to meet her gaze. "How about you start by not forcing me to go to cooking camp?"

The last traces of patience evaporated from my mother's face. My shoulders slumped in defeat. I've always had this bad habit of not knowing when to stop till it's too late. Maybe that was something else I got from Papa.

"Right, then," Mombo said, clapping her hands onto the steering wheel. "Off you go. Don't want to be late on your first day. You're in room 113."

"Of all the numbers," I muttered.

With a groan, I clicked off my seatbelt, lifted Webster into my backpack, and slid out of the car. I had my lunch bag in one hand and my backpack over my shoulder. Webster's head was poking out from the unzipped top and he was chattering loudly. Complaining to me about the car ride. He's never liked them. Probably thinks we're taking him to the vet.

I closed my eyes and spun around seven times, slowly so I wouldn't get dizzy. I was going to need as much luck as possible to get me through this day!

"Love you, darling," Mombo said with a fluttery wave, her perfectly manicured pinky finger politely extended. My mother could give the Queen lessons in daintiness.

"*Ciao,*" I muttered. But not quite loud enough for her to hear.

Once her car was out of sight, I turned around and dragged my feet into the building, past the info desk, and down the main hall in search of room 113. It wasn't even nine o'clock yet but the air outside was already thick with humidity.

It had been way too hot to sleep last night, even with all the windows open and the big electric fan running on high beside my bed, so I'd gotten up at sunrise to take Webster down to the harbour for a cool dip. I try my best to take him swimming at least once a day, except in the winter when the water's icy and he has to make do with our bathtub. Mombo thinks we should keep Webster connected to his duck roots as much as possible so he won't suffer from species-identity-loss. Sometimes we'll see other ducks at the shore and I always encourage him to go play and make friends. But he never does and I don't want to force him. Gotta admit, I secretly love the fact that he prefers me to his own species.

This morning while Webster was paddling around the harbour, I searched up the FindYourPeeps app on my brand-new-old phone. The screen froze on the search page for so long, I worried I'd broken it on my very first try. Cell signals in the Spot aren't exactly the strongest, but still. And then I started to wonder if the glitching was a sign I shouldn't be doing what I was doing. Were the powers of the internet telling me to turn back? That maybe I wasn't going to like what I was about to find? That maybe my mother had a good reason for shutting down all my questions about Papa? But I'd been waiting for months to get this app. How could I turn back now? Mombo and I shared a computer at home so it's not like I could search for him there. But then suddenly there was a flicker and the screen filled with words.

FindYourPeeps
(for Mobile Phones)
Are you searching for a long-lost friend?
Yearning to reconnect with a missing relative?

Search no more! We're here to help!

I'd clicked the *get* button after checking over my shoulder. I was so worried somebody might see me. Although really, the only person who'd be mad would be Mombo. And possibly Gran. But I was prepared to take my chances. I needed to do this. And I needed to do it now. The ten-year anniversary of the day he left was coming up. I was done with waiting.

I trudged past the library and the daycare and the vending machine, until finally I was standing outside the door of room 113. There was a funny smell coming from inside. I sniffed the air a few times but couldn't figure it out. I glanced back at Webster.

"You ready for this?" I asked, hiking up my backpack.

He leaned his cheek against mine and clucked twice. That meant *yes*.

Or *si* in Italian.

Deep breaths.

"Okay, then. *Andiamo*," I said, taking a step forward and pushing open the door.

Exploring Zee Joy

The door closed behind us with a *snick*. I stood stone-still for a few seconds, taking in the details from behind my shaggy bangs.

We were standing in an oversized kitchen with low ceilings, dim tube lighting and shiny peeling paint that looked so much like mayonnaise I suddenly found myself craving a tuna sandwich. There was a low wooden desk at the front near the door, and a wall of floor-to-ceiling cupboards at the back — the pantry, I figured. In between was a fridge, a pair of ovens, and a long grey island with a sink at each end. A sharp aroma hung in the air like a stinky fog. Burnt cheese, I think. How many epic cooking disasters have these mayonnaise walls witnessed over the years?

Two kids stood on opposite ends of the island. I recognized them immediately because . . . sorry, did I mention how the Spot only has one middle school? The girl with the red-streaked blond pigtails and the leave-me-alone scowl was the infamous Madz Schipper — new kid this year and one of those notable exceptions I was

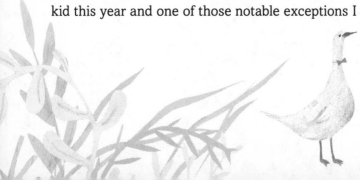

mentioning earlier. Her family had moved here from Toronto at the beginning of February, which was all anyone could talk about for months afterward because:

1. Nobody new ever moves to this town. Especially not in the middle of winter.

and

2. This was about as exciting as things get around here.

She always wore black clothes and owned a seemingly never-ending supply of snarky graphic T-shirts. She spent every lunch period by herself in the library and she had a little brother in the first grade. That's about all I could tell you about her. She's in my class, but we've never actually spoken. I would though. If she wasn't so scary.

The other kid, with the glasses and carrot-coloured flippy hair was JD Granger. He's in the grade above mine and the closest thing to a celebrity our school has. Not only had he won the BBTS PS student council vice presidential nomination for the coming school year, he finished seventh grade as head of the eco team, the debate team and the dance and yearbook committees. He was also lead trumpet in the school band. Oh, and he was in a really famous soda pop commercial a couple of years ago. You've probably seen it.

The two of them were watching me and Webster warily, like we were a pair of grenades about to go off. After all these years, Webster and I should have been used to people staring at us. My grip tightened around the straps of my backpack.

"Um, hi," I said forcing out a half-hearted smile.

Neither of them replied. Trying my best to look cool with a duck on my back, I walked across the room, lifted Webster from the backpack, and settled him down on his favourite travel blanket in the corner of the room, beside one of the windows.

"Be a good boy, okay?" I whispered, giving him half a Cheerio from my pocket. He gobbled it up, shook his feathers out, circled three times, and sat down.

I shuffled back to the island and took a spot in front of a dusty spice rack at the very middle. A place as perfectly equidistant as possible from the other two kids, who still hadn't said anything yet.

A prickly silence bubbled up around us. Were we just going to stand here until the rest of the kids arrived? I figured I should probably give the conversation thing one more shot. That way, when I told Mombo how much I hated camp at the end of the day, she couldn't legitimately accuse me of not trying.

I turned to my left, where the girl was busily picking

at her fingernails. Her black T-shirt of the day read *Sass Dealer.*

"Madison, right?" I asked, swallowing the sticky lump of nerves in my throat.

She rolled her eyes and flicked some chipped-off inky nail polish into the sink beside her. Lovely.

There was a tap on my shoulder. I spun around and came face-to-face with JD. Well, almost. He was tall. But not quite as tall as me. "You're second violin," he declared proudly, like he just got the right answer on a pop quiz.

I was surprised he'd noticed. Strings and horns don't mix much in the music room. "Good memory."

"That your duck?"

"Yeah."

"Nice," he said, like it was exactly the kind of answer he heard all the time. "I've seen you walking him around town. So . . . you a Dumbo fan or what?"

My cheeks flushed with heat. "Sorry?"

He adjusted the position of his glasses and gestured toward my stomach. I glanced down.

"Actually, this is Babar," I corrected him. "You know, from the books?" It was my luckiest T-shirt and one of my favourite pieces from my collection. At last count, I had 349 elephants — not real ones, of course. Mostly stuffed animals, figurines, jewellery, shirts, a couple of hats and even an elephant desk lamp I had named Alfredo. It all started when I got an elephant charm bracelet as a present from Gran on my seventh birthday. It was really old and very special — she got it as a gift from an aunt who had travelled to Thailand when she was a kid. Apparently, elephants are good luck. I figured a kid like me could use as much luck as possible in this world, so I decided to start an elephant collection. I also collect travel posters. When I finally get a passport, I'm definitely going to do a safari so I can visit some real live elephants in their natural habitat.

Fortunately, JD didn't get a chance to ask any more nosy questions, because a second later, the door opened with a *whoosh* and in walked a woman in a red sundress and gold sandals. She had tanned skin and a mane of long, black hair, dark false eyelashes, and a bright, wide, red-lipsticked smile. She looked like she could be a shampoo model. Or a toothpaste spokesperson. And she seemed really young. Like, barely old enough to be finished with high school. Not at all how I imagined a fancy flown-in-from-Paris chef would look. Shouldn't she at least be wearing one of those dorky-looking, floppy white hats? She dropped her bag onto the desk and turned to face us.

"Hello *bonjour*, I am happy to see everyone has arrived on time. Punctuality is *très* important."

I glanced around. This is *everyone*?

"I welcome you to my class, where we will explore the joy of French cuisine together. My name is Giselle Leblanc, but you may call me Chef Gigi. By the end of this week, you will have the skills to prepare a true feast. All your families will join us. Good, yes?"

She clapped her hands happily like she was giving herself a round of applause. JD clapped along with her, and Gigi flashed him a bright, big-toothed smile in return. "Excellent. Now, when I say your name, please come forward and collect a recipe book and apron. And if you please, tell us something about yourself."

I had to listen really carefully to follow what this lady was saying. Her accent was so strong and she kept saying *zee* instead of *the* and *zis* instead of *this*. And was it just me, or didn't French people pronounce the letter *h*? She opened her bag, dug out a sheet of paper and a pen, and plopped herself down on the chair. "Joshua Granger?" she said, scanning the room.

"JD" he said, marching up to the desk and holding out his hand, very business-like. "Incoming VP of the BBTS PS student council and future Prime Minister."

"Ah. Very nice to meet you." Gigi shook his hand,

looking impressed. Blah. Did I mention JD was also head of our school's young politicians club?

"Madeline Schipper?"

Ooof. Did I just call her Madison?

"I only answer to Madz. With a *z*," she said, stomping past me to collect her apron. "And I like black. Does this come in any other colours?"

"*Non.*"

Madz's scowl grew so harsh, I thought she might sprain a face muscle. She returned to her place by the sink, holding the bright red apron out in front of her like a bag of garbage.

"Sarah Lasagna?"

"Yes. Uh . . . present." Maybe I should request a nickname too? I took my time making my way up to Gigi's desk, my brain scrambling to come up with a good alternative for Sarah.

Sar? Sarry? Sariah?

Crumb.

I decided against shaking her hand or anything cringey like that. "I think it's only fair to tell you," I whispered, "that I am here under duress." I picked up my recipe folder and apron. "Are you really from Paris?"

She smiled brightly. "Yes, of course."

"What's it like?"

"*Très belle.* Like a painting."

I sighed wistfully and looped the apron around my neck. As I returned to my spot by the spice rack, I thought about how wearing an apron made me feel weirdly like my mother. But not necessarily in a good way.

JD smirked as I passed him. "Lasagna? Really?"

"It's Italian," I sniffed.

"So, what's your middle name? Macaroni?"

"How original," I said, wishing so badly I had something witty to retort. Like, *What does the* D *stand for? Doofus?* But by the time I thought of that, it was too late to qualify as clever. And I didn't really have the guts to say it anyway.

As I was fastening the apron ties around my back, I took a quick peek over at Webster to make sure he was okay. He'd fallen asleep and was snoring softly with his beak tucked under his wing. My heart always melted a little when he did that. But a second later, he startled awake when Gigi stood up and began talking. Actually, it was more like yelling. With a French accent.

"Turn to page eight in your recipe book," she commanded. "We begin our cooking lessons with a basic but traditional French dish. Zee crepes!"

Crepes? Isn't that just a fancy name for pancakes? I

was flipping through the book when there was another tap on my shoulder.

"Psst. Hey, Mac?" I pretended not to notice. But the tapping continued. Sheesh. JD was as persistent as a hungry mosquito. "Don't want to alarm you, but I think you're in the wrong room," he hissed.

I dropped the folder and glanced around the kitchen. "What do you mean?"

"Didn't you see the sign?" he asked, grinning so widely I could see his molars. "Spaghetti camp is down the hall." He snorted twice, then erupted into a laughing fit.

For the second time that morning, I felt my cheeks flooding with heat. "Very funny," I said, turning my attention back to the book. And for the bazillionth time since last night, I mentally cursed Helen and her broken ankle and Mombo for ruining my birthday week and forcing me and Webster to come to this camp.

"Let us cook," Gigi said, walking toward us with a stack of metal mixing bowls. "To begin, everyone will need milk, butter and eggs. And please find a, how do you say . . . whisk, and—*aaaaaaah!*"

There was a loud clatter as the bowls crashed to the floor. I jumped and turned to look in alarm. Gigi was clutching the counter like it was the only thing holding her up. Her eyes were as round as dinner plates.

"Mon Dieu!" she screeched. "What is *zat*?"

Before I knew what was happening, she'd grabbed a wooden spoon off the counter and held it out in front of her like a sword.

Her hand was trembling as she pointed it right at Webster.

"Open the window!" she cried.

And then she charged.

Friend or Food?

"Wait!" I cried, throwing myself in front of Webster, arms spread wide like a human stop sign. "What are you doing?"

Gigi crouched low as a wrestler, ready to attack. Her breathing was panicky and her wooden spoon was wavering just inches from my face. "Move aside while I shoo the beast out!" She snapped her fingers. "The window! Now!"

There was a ruffle of feathers and a whole lot of agitated quacking coming from behind me. "What? No!" I bent down and scooped Webster up. His little body trembled in my arms. I held him tight and stroked his feathers, trying to calm him down. Poor baby. We've had our fair share of strange looks over the years, but nobody's ever tried to shoo him out a window before. "He's mine!"

Her eyes narrowed. "Eh? What does this mean?" she asked, lowering the spoon slightly.

"His name is Webster," I explained, stroking his head gently. "See, he's very well-behaved. My mother

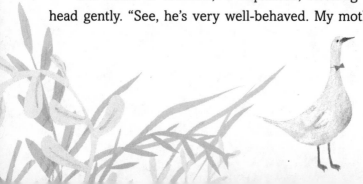

called ahead and got permission from the camp. He's allowed to be here."

Gigi's nose wrinkled like she'd just stepped in fresh dog poop. *"Absolument non!* I have not come all the way from Paris for this!"

"He won't be any trouble. I promise. Everyone in the Spot loves—"

"Non! No ducks!"

"But, he's hypoallergenic. And very clean. Look, he even wears a diaper."

For some reason, that just seemed to upset her even more. She shook her finger at us, letting loose a tsunami of what sounded like French.

"Excuse me," I said, suddenly wishing I'd paid more attention to Mademoiselle Schwartz's lessons this year. "Please . . . I . . . I don't understand . . . What are you saying?"

She switched back into English, as easily as changing shoes. "In France, ducks are meant to be on the plate. Not. In. The. *Class!"*

"W-what do you mean?" I felt like I'd been pelted with a bucketful of ice chips. I glanced around the room, looking for help. JD and Madz were standing like a pair of statues, watching us in silent shock.

"This animal," she said, pointing a finger at

Webster's beak, "is an ingredient. Not a pet!"

Was this really happening? It felt like some kind of crazy dream I might have after eating too many slices of double-pepperoni and onion pizza for dinner. I turned back to Chef Gigi, trying to find the words that would make her understand what Webster meant to me. "You can't *cook* him," I said, hot tears beginning to pool in my eyes. "He is . . . He's my best friend." My voice crumbled over this last part and I dropped my chin onto his little head. There was a shuffling of feet and a swirl of air and the next thing I knew, Madz and JD were standing on either side of me.

An apron-clad army of three. Plus a duck.

"Chill out, Cheffy," said Madz, whose perma-scowl had been replaced by a look of defiance. "Webster's cool — why don't you give him a chance? Everyone in this town seems to love him."

Except for Jill and Ms. Petri, I thought. But this probably wasn't the best moment to point that out.

Gigi looked like she was about to reply but JD cut in first. "Legally speaking, I have to wonder how the community centre management will feel when they see video footage of an employee violently threatening the life of an innocent animal." He held up his phone and waggled it devilishly.

Gigi's jaw dropped. She was speechless for a few glorious seconds before she threw the spoon onto the counter and started yelling again. *"Incroyable!* Pet ducks in my kitchen? Now I have seen everything!" She whipped her own phone out of her apron pocket and stomped toward the door. "This was not in my contract! *Excusez-moi."* With a whoosh and a slam, she was gone.

Madz let out a whoop of triumph. "Girl, bye," she said with a flip of her hand. It was the first time I'd ever seen her crack a smile. It looked good on her. Her teeth were small and sharp looking, like a cat.

I took a few deep breaths, hugging Webster tightly and waiting for my heart rate to calm down. At least he wasn't trembling anymore. "Thanks for helping," I said after a minute.

JD play-punched me in the arm. "No worries, Mac," he said.

I bristled but decided to let this one go. "Did you really get her on video?"

"Nope," he said, popping his phone back into the pocket of his shorts. "Pretty convincing though, eh? My agent would have been proud."

I had to admit, I was impressed. "Wow. Yeah, I totally bought it."

"Me too," Madz said, stalking off in the direction of

the fridge. "*Très* Oscar-worthy."

JD took off his glasses and gave them a quick polish with the hem of his apron. "So, your duck's name is Webster?"

"Yeah, well, you know, because of his feet," I said, settling him back down on his blanket. "They're webbed."

I stood back up to see JD watching me with a know-it-all smirk plastered on his face. "How original."

My cheeks flashed with heat. "Hey. I was two."

"I guess we should all be glad you didn't name him Ravioli."

I tried my best to look unimpressed while I scrambled to come up with a clever reply. Pasta jokes had been the bane of my existence since the day I started kindergarten. You'd think I'd be better at deflecting them by now. "Huh. Like I haven't heard that one a hundred times," I finally said, hopefully not too late to sting.

Spinning on my heel, I returned to my spot in front of the spice rack and dug my phone out of my back pocket. That app had still been loading last time I looked. This felt like as good a time as any to check to see if it was done.

My stomach did a flip when I saw it waiting there for me on my screen. I took a deep breath, stabbed the *open* tab and scanned my eyes down the splash page.

Welcome to the FindYourPeeps Network Corp Ltd.
Let's get started!

In order to conduct a successful search, please gather as much of the following information as possible on your missing loved one.

Remember, the more details you give us, the quicker we can complete your re-connection.

I scrolled down, down, down the screen. The list of requested information seemed to go on forever and I could feel all my excitement draining away line by line. *Full name. Birthday. Place of birth. Parents' names. Cities of residence. Height. Weight. Distinctive Features. Nicknames. Aliases. Hobbies and interests. Teams or clubs. Education. Last known place of employment.*

Jeepers. There was so much I didn't know. All I had was a last name and birth country. This was going to be way harder than I thought.

Out of the corner of my eye, I saw JD striding toward me. I quickly clicked off my phone, picked up my recipe folder and pretended to read about crepes. "Don't you have some whisking to do?" I asked.

"Hard pass. I don't whisk without direct instructions."

That made sense. With Gigi gone, none of us seemed especially interested in cooking. Eating, though, was clearly another story. Madz's entire head was in the fridge and I could hear her rummaging around, clinking bottles and jars, opening drawers. "You guys! There's chocolate sauce!" She cried, pulling out a tall plastic container. She flicked open the lid and squirted a long, dark stream right into her mouth.

"Um . . . should you be doing that?" I asked.

"Why not?" she said, licking her lips before gleefully squirting herself another shot of sauce. "Cheffy's not here."

My eyes skipped over to the door. "But she could come back any second."

Madz shrugged. Her lips and chin were drizzled in a layer of chocolate syrup. An almost-perfect match for her T-shirt. "Haven't you ever coloured outside the lines, Lasagna?"

"Yeah, of course . . . but—"

"Well then, how is this any different? I mean, it's not our fault the instructor left us, three helpless young children, completely unsupervised. And hungry. In a fully stocked kitchen." She took a final squirt, snapped the cap back on, and returned her head to the fridge. There were a few more seconds of clinking before she pulled out a can of whipped cream. Her eyes sparked with mischief.

JD walked to the window, cupped his hands around his eyes, and peered between the slats. "Um, I don't think she's coming back anytime soon."

"Why?"

He waved me over. "See for yourself."

Reluctantly, I joined him at the window and peered out. There was Chef Gigi, pacing in circles around the parking lot.

She was talking on her phone and gesturing furiously with her free hand. Every now and then, she'd pause and stomp a gold-sandalled foot in anger. We couldn't make out what she was saying, but whoever she was speaking to was getting quite an earful. All I could think was, *better them than us*.

"Hey guys," Madz called. We turned around to find her standing by the door, holding up what looked to be a brick of cheese. "Let's go exploring."

"What?" I squeaked in surprise. I don't remember seeing her do anything this rebellious in school. All that chocolate and whipped cream must have gone straight to her head. "We'll get in trouble."

Gripping the cheese between her teeth, she untied her apron and volleyed it into the nearest sink.

"Only if she catches us," she said, biting off a hunk. Her mouth was so full of cheese, she could barely pull her lips closed. My mother would have a cow if I ever ate with such bad manners.

JD's apron sailed through the air right over my head, joining Madz's in the sink. He made a beeline for the door.

"Hurry up, Mac," he shouted over his shoulder. "Let's go!"

To my complete and utter surprise, I only hesitated for a second.

Be Like a Duck

Way back when I was little and Grandad was teaching me how to swim and I was a splashy, spluttericious mess of floaty wings and flailing arms and legs, he pulled me to the side of the pool and said something that made a lot of sense.

"You take Webster swimming every day, right?

"Yeah," I'd replied.

"And so you can picture how he does it, right?"

"Yeah."

"Okay. So now, hold that image in your head and try to *be like him*. Calm on the surface, but always paddling furiously underneath. That's the way to do it."

I tried my best. Ducks make it look so easy, but it's really hard work. Webster's lucky, he was born that way. I'm twelve now and I still haven't completely figured out how to pull it off. But I think about it a lot.

Be like a duck.

It's good advice for all of us.

And not just for swimming.

Where Beaches Go

I dropped into the passenger seat with Webster and yanked the door closed with a thundiferous *whump*.

Mombo winced and studied my face. "Oh, darling. It couldn't have been all that bad."

"Worst. Day. Ever."

Okay, so maybe that was an exaggeration. But I was in a bratty mood and wanted her to feel guilty. I mean, poor Webster was cruelly labelled an *ingredient* by a snooty French chef. Not to mention threatened with a wooden spoon! Although in the end, I have to admit, the day sort of turned out okay.

It was pretty awkward at first, but a few minutes into our "exploring" mission we ran across a vending machine, and since JD happened to have a pocketful of spare change, he bought us all a boatload of chips and chocolate bars and soda pop. And after all that sugar and junk food, the three of us started feeling pretty bouncy. We ended up racing each other around the halls of the community centre's second floor. With Webster cheering me on, I won all the races. Every single one.

Guess that's one of the bonuses of having super-long legs. JD tried not to show it, but I could tell he was furious. Which I thought was perfect payback for all his stupid pasta jokes.

We got bored of racing and went back to room 113 after about half an hour. But Chef Gigi hadn't come back yet. So we sat on the floor and played spit with the miniature deck of cards I kept in the side pocket of my backpack for boredom emergencies — although until that moment, I had only ever played solitaire with them. I'd never been the kind of kid who made friends easily. So the fact that both JD and Madz actually seemed to be enjoying my company took me by surprise. Saving Webster from that spoon attack must have been a more intense bonding moment than I realized.

By the time Gigi finally returned from the parking lot, she refused to look me in the eye but announced that "the beast" could stay if he kept far away from the food preparation areas. #epicwinforTeamWebster

Whoop whoop! But after all that, there was only enough time left to make one batch of crepes, which broke apart when we flipped them so we had to throw them all into the compost bin. Good thing they told us to bring our own lunches!

#epicflopforCheffy

I didn't care too much anyway since I was still full from all the junk food. But I'm sure Gigi secretly blamed it on Webster.

"Ugh. Why's it so hot in here?" I asked, fiddling with the temperature dials on the dashboard.

"I can't get the A/C to turn on. I think it's probably on the fritz. Just roll down your window."

"Super."

"Were the other kids nice at least? Did you make any friends?"

I shrugged, not sure I was ready to give her the satisfaction of knowing that JD and Madz were actually kind of okay.

"Maybe you'll tell me more about it over dinner? We can make those special smoothies of yours if you want. Maybe watch a movie?" She released the parking brake and started to drive while I rolled my window down to release some of the trapped heat of the car.

"But do you mind if we make a quick stop at the beach house to see how your grandfather is feeling?" she asked. "I brought him some chicken soup from the shop."

"I thought he needed peace and quiet?"

"Yes. But apparently a very quick visit would be acceptable."

"Fine by me," I replied, even though this wasn't exactly chicken soup weather. Today was hot enough to melt an entire ice cream truck.

A few minutes later, with Webster in my arms and a pair of soup-filled thermoses in Mombo's, we climbed the stone steps leading to the front door of my grandparents' beach house — which is what Gran calls a "misnomer," since there isn't a beach anywhere in sight. Well, not anymore, at least. Grandad likes to tell the story of the day the Spot's beach disappeared all those years ago in a storm. "One day it was there, the next it was gone. Just like that."

I've always found that a little hard to believe but Mombo says she's seen old pictures of the missing beach, although she was just a baby when it supposedly vanished. Looking out across the shore, it's hard to imagine a beautiful sandy beach was ever there. Now it's all just rock pools, crushed shells and craggy stone. Why would a storm want to steal a beach anyway? And where would it go?

Sometimes I imagined our missing beach floating willy-nilly around the ocean, trying desperately to find its way home. Or planning a forbidden rendezvous with some exotic, faraway sandbar. But really, it's probably more likely that our beach just got sick of us and wanted to move to another town. Somewhere more exciting. Or even just a place with a nicer name.

The moment we stepped inside the house, a blanket of perfectly chilled, lemon-scented air surrounded us. My grandparents' air conditioner was clearly working just fine. I inhaled the delicious coolness, thinking of the sticky, gross heat that would be greeting us back at home.

"Did they at least come to fix our apartment A/C today?"

"No. Apparently nobody's available to come until Friday."

Four more nights in that sauna? Ugh. "Wouldn't it be nice if we could just sleep here tonight instead?" I whispered. "I mean, since our special week's not happening the way it's supposed to."

Mombo wagged her finger at me. "Be careful what you wish for, darling," she whispered back. "And watch for the signal, okay?"

The signal was something we came up with a long time ago. A double-ear whisk with your pinky finger meant time for a quick exit. We've used it a bunch of times over the years, but mostly when we're visiting Gran.

She was waiting for us in the kitchen. This place

used to be their summer cottage, back in the days when there was a pretty beach and a nice view. They also had a house in the city where they lived the rest of the year. But after Mombo and I were on our own, they retired and moved here full-time to be near their only child and grandchild (#thatwouldbeme).

It was still decorated like a vacation home, with seashell wallpaper, anchor-printed curtains and nautical artwork everywhere you turned. I fixed my gaze on the cheesy grinning whale print hanging on the wall beside the window and for the eleventy-billionth time, heard myself thinking *why*? It's not like my grandparents can't afford nice things. I know this for a fact.

Their old brown pug, Lola, scampered over and sniffed my toes. Gran waved me over for a kiss.

"Hello, Caroline. Hello, Sarah."

"Hi, Gran," I said, leaning down slightly so her lips could reach my cheek.

The smell of her peppermint-scented arthritis cream filled my nose. Her kiss was so dry and light, it felt like a feather brushing over my skin.

"How was the rest of your birthday, darling?"

"Fine, thanks. I got a cell phone."

"Did you really?" She fixed her steely blue eyes on Mombo and smiled stiffly. "Caroline, how very modern of you. I certainly wouldn't have placed that kind of advanced technology in *your* hands when you were at the very tender age of twelve."

"Maybe because cell phones hadn't been invented back then, Mother?" she said, sweeping past her as she set the thermoses down on the counter. "I brought soup for Dad."

Gran picked them up and walked them over to the fridge. "Even so. Sarah's still just a child, you know. A phone is a big responsibility."

"That soup is still hot," Mombo said, plucking the thermoses off the fridge shelf and hip-checking the door shut. "You can't refrigerate it just yet."

"It seals in the flavour," Gran replied, reaching to take the thermoses back. "Not to mention the nutrients. Much healthier for you. I hope you'll be monitoring her activities on that thing."

"That's an old wives' tale," Mombo said, holding the thermoses over her head.

Gran tapped her loafer impatiently. "Well, I'm an old wife. Besides, I'd rather not have hot soup ring stains on my countertops."

"Then why don't we just serve it now?"

"It's too early for dinner!"

I backed up, clutching Webster tightly. He pecked at

my T-shirt and let out a reassuring peep. We both knew there was an epic argument brewing.

"Sarah? Is that you?"

"Hey, Grandad," I said, escaping into the living room with Webster still in my arms.

My grandfather was sitting in his favourite armchair by the picture window, reading something on his iPad. It was funny to see him dressed in a bathrobe and slippers this late in the afternoon. The curtains over the window were closed. Gran didn't like looking out on the ugliness where the beach used to be, so she usually insisted on keeping them shut. Even on sunny days.

"How's your hernia?" I asked, bending down to give him a one-arm hug. I tried to be careful not to squeeze too tight.

"All fixed up, thanks. I'll be back to my fighting shape in a few days."

I giggled at the thought of my silver-haired, pot-bellied grandfather bouncing around a boxing ring.

"Goodness, my dear," he said, pulling off his reading glasses. "Did you get taller again?"

"Very possibly," I replied faintly. One of my secret fears was that I was going to be stuck in a growth spurt forever and end up the tallest girl in the history of the universe. This was not an exaggeration.

"I hear you're attending a cooking camp. How was your first day?"

I stroked Webster's neck while I considered how to answer. "It was okay, I guess . . ."

"Your Gran and I are looking forward to that big feast at the end of the week." He smiled and ran a hand lightly over his pot-belly. "I insist on being all healed up by then."

"No really, Grandad. You guys don't have to come—"

"Nonsense! We wouldn't miss it for the world." He patted my arm proudly. "I'll be sure to bring my appetite."

I opened my mouth to reply, but nothing came out.

"Hey, I got you a birthday present," he said, reaching into the pocket of his robe and pulling out a small box. Inside was a necklace with a tiny silver elephant hanging from a chain. I let out a squeak of happiness. *Three hundred and fifty!*

"I love it. You're the best, Grandad!" I said, putting Webster down on his lap so I could fasten the clasp around my neck.

This was not an exaggeration either. He really is the best. Over the years, he's taught me how to ride a bike and climb a tree, how to do the side stroke, and swan dive off the high board. How to catch a worm, how to find a geode, and how to identify the different kinds of sea life inside a tide pool. Baseball is his favourite sport and he insisted on teaching me how to hit a line drive up the middle and make a diving catch in the outfield. And every year on Father's Day, we spend the day fishing — just him, me and Webster. Would my actual father know how to do half the amazing things Grandad did? Or even one of them? I had no idea. My thoughts skipped back to that list from FindMyPeeps: *Place of birth. Hobbies and Interests. Education . . .*

"Hey, this might sound like a strange question but . . ." I took a deep breath. ". . . Do you happen to know where in Italy Papa was from?"

Grandad's eyebrows shot up. The deep folds that made in his forehead reminded me of an accordion. "Why are you asking?"

"It's . . . well . . . we're doing a project on Italy for school."

"I thought classes didn't begin until next week?"

"I'm, uh . . . just hoping to get a head start."

"Atta girl," he said, patting my knee.

"So? Do you know the name of the city? Or town? Or . . . whatever?"

Jeepers, why did I suddenly feel like a criminal? But I knew the answer before I was even finished thinking the words. Because if Mombo knew what I was doing, she'd probably never forgive me.

"Oh, goodness. I'd have to give it some thought. Somewhere in the south, if memory serves."

Somewhere in the south? That was probably way too vague to be much help. "Do you know if he—"

"Hello? What are you two whispering about in here?"

I spun around to see Mombo and Gran standing right behind me.

Crumble.

Seven Things You Should Know about Gran

1. She has grandma hobbies.

Like knitting. And golf. But her very favourite one is criticizing my mother while disguising it as constructive parenting advice. I know Gran means well. She's always felt like a second mother to me, especially since Papa left. When I was little, she watched over me every day while Mombo went to work. Which means we got a chance to know each other pretty well over the years. I love her and all but, just between you and me, she's utterly bananas.

2. She collects weird stuff.

Like stamps. And empty perfume bottles. And teeny-tiny useless silver teaspoons. No, that last one is not a joke. She keeps dozens of those spoons in these wooden cases hanging on the wall of the dining room. Every time she travels anywhere — even just a neighbouring town — she has to buy another one for her collection. It's like an addiction. And last year she had to go out and buy a third case because the first and second ones were starting to overflow. I asked her once what the point of all those spoons were since they were clearly way too small to actually eat anything with, if they ever got a chance to come down off the wall, that is. But she just replied: "the usefulness of a cup is in its emptiness."

See what I mean?

Bananas.

3. She yells a lot.

4. She drives like a daredevil.

5. She's rich but really cheap.

You should see the way she can make a single tea bag stretch for a whole week. She even got married in a black dress so she could wear it again to cocktail parties.

6. She's obsessively neat and loves to seek out messes (specifically mine) so she can complain about them (specifically to Mombo).

Which I'm sure is the reason she and Webster have never gotten along. Every time I'd forget to clean up the footprints he sometimes left on the floor, watch out! She'd threaten to pluck him and make a pillow out of his feathers if I didn't smarten up. I've never understood what being smart has to do with cleaning the floor, and I'm pretty sure Gran wasn't actually serious about the pillow thing. But I don't want to take the chance.

7. *She helps keep Mombo's secrets.*
About Papa.
From me.

Doctor's Orders

"Oh, hi," I gasped. "I didn't see you there."

"We thought you two might be hungry," Gran said, narrowing her eyes suspiciously. She was holding a plate of ginger cookies in one hand and a bowl of grapes in the other. Mombo carried a tray with lemonade and four empty glasses and a small dish of frozen peas, which were Webster's favourite. Looks like they agreed to disagree on serving the chicken soup. "Did we interrupt an important conversation?"

"Well, uh . . . We . . ."

Usually whenever anybody asks me a question I don't like, I handle it by giving them an answer to a completely different question. This is an excellent strategy to throw nosy people off track and it usually works pretty well. Unfortunately, it's not easy coming up with alternate words when you feel like someone's just dropped a giant rock into the pit of your stomach. "You see . . . I was just . . . um . . ."

"Yes, you did interrupt us, Lillian," Grandad cut in. "But it's quite all right. Sarah was just telling me how

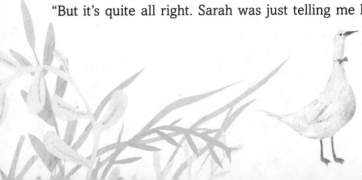

much she was looking forward to the new school year."

Phew! Nice save, I thought, letting out the giant breath I'd been holding. I shot him a quick thank-you smile.

"Oh, how lovely," Gran said, putting the plates down on the coffee table. "But darling, I don't think that bird should be on your lap. You're still recovering from surgery and who knows what kind of germs it's carrying." She turned her attention to my mother. "Caroline, didn't you explain to your daughter about the doctor's orders?"

"She did. Sorry," I said, scooping Webster up quickly and carrying him to the other side of the room. "But please, Webster is a *he* . . . not an *it*. He's sensitive about that kind of thing."

Gran snorted. "How exactly can a duck—"

"Mother, please," Mombo cut in. "Can we drop it?"

Gran rolled her eyes and straightened the hem of her cashmere cardigan over her waist. "Well *he* has just left a trail of footprints on my clean floor."

I sighed. Mombo was right. The idea of going home to our overheated apartment was sounding pretty darn wonderful right about now. "I'll wipe them up, don't worry."

"Good. Come have a cookie. Or two. You're so thin, I can practically see right through you."

"Okay," I said, grabbing one off the plate.

"But eat it quickly because it's getting late and you don't want to spoil your dinner."

I knew better than to let on that Mombo had promised monster marshmallow smoothies for dinner and there was no way on earth anything could possibly spoil that. "Got it," I said, stuffing the cookie into my mouth and trying my best to keep my lips closed while I chewed it, which was not as easy as it might sound. The fact that it was stale didn't help.

"Not that quickly!" Gran snapped. "For goodness sake, didn't your mother teach you any manners?"

"Yefpth," I replied, covering my mouth to catch the spray of crumbs. Webster waddled over to nibble them up but Lola got there first and snaffled them all. Grandad raised a hand to cover the look of amusement spreading across his face. *Why, oh why, couldn't I have inherited just a few of Mombo's dainty genes?* I bet Gran would have liked me better then. I turned slightly, trying my best to chew and swallow that dry cookie with as many manners as I could remember.

My eyes landed on the ugly pink-and-orange seashell painting hanging beside the bookcase, and my thoughts rewound back to that day last year when Gran had shown me a painting that she said was one of her most "prized possessions." It had been given to her by an artist friend of hers way back in the olden days when they were young and before he had become famous. And absolutely before she married Grandad (she made sure to point out). Which made me wonder if the artist had been her boyfriend. She kept it covered in bubble wrap and hidden under her bed. When she pulled it out to show it to me, I was rattled. I wanted to ask her why she was hiding a beautiful painting away where nobody could see it. But then I thought that question might annoy her. Clearly, she believed the dark, dusty sliver of space under her bed was the right place for it. And what did I know about art anyway?

I burped as politely as humanly possible when my ordeal with the stale cookie was finally over. But apparently it wasn't polite enough 'cause Gran frowned and opened her mouth to let out a fresh load of complaining. Luckily, Mombo noticed in time.

"Gosh, Mother — it's getting late," she cut in, her pinky finger whisking wild circles around the inside of her ear. "We really should get going. I've got a big dinner planned."

Dear Papa,

I don't remember the day you left. I just remember being sad that you were gone. Mombo told me you were away on a long business trip because I asked *Where's Papa now?* for years afterwards. It was the only time she ever talked about you, so I asked a lot. Like, every day. And she always gave me a different answer.

Well, I believe today he's got a meeting in Timbuktu . . . He just landed in Reykjavik . . . He's finalizing a deal near Mount Kilimanjaro . . . At a conference in Constantinople . . .

You get the idea. Then we'd go pull out the atlas and I'd see if I could pinpoint your latest destination. We either ran out of new places to find or maybe I just lost interest in the game, because eventually a day came when we tucked the atlas away on a high shelf in the living room — the one Mombo needs a stepladder to reach. That must have been when I figured out you weren't going to walk back into our lives any time soon. After that, we didn't talk about you anymore. But I think about you every day. And I wonder what a little kid could have done that was so horrible to make a father want to leave and never come back.

The few memories I have of you are like a handful

of blurry photographs. Dark, curly hair. Glasses. Riding around on big, sturdy shoulders. Suntanned hands picking me up and swinging me around while we danced with Mombo in our living room.

What do you remember about me?

Sometimes you visit in my dreams. Even though your face is fuzzy, I always know it's you by your deep voice and the sea salt smell on your skin. You speak to me in words I can't understand but I figure must be Italian. Sometimes you sing. I used to try telling Mombo about those dreams but I stopped a few years back. Whenever I mention you, she shuts the conversation down. Fast.

Today I downloaded another app on my new-old phone. This one's called FindYourPeeps.

So . . .

Prepare to be found.

Your daughter,
Sarah

Thoughts that Keep Me Up at Night Sometimes

1. What if I never stop growing and am forced to live my adult life in a custom-built giraffe-style house with an adjustable roof?

2. What if Mombo gets remarried to someone I don't like and I have to share my room with a pair of evil stepsisters who boss me around and make me do their chores?

3. What if the world comes to an end before I ever get a chance to fly on a plane? Or fall in love? Or ride an elephant? Or find Papa?

4. What if he left because of me?

Cheesed

Chef Gigi was pacing the hall outside room 113, jabbering away on her phone — a stream of turbo-speed chatter with hand gestures to match — when I arrived at the community centre the next morning. She barely made time to breathe between sentences. I don't even think she saw me and Webster pass by on our way into the class. I settled Webster on his blanket and took my place at the island.

"Who's she talking to out there?" I asked, fastening my apron.

JD shrugged. "Dunno. I'm guessing maybe her boyfriend."

"Yeah," Madz added, "I eavesdropped for a minute and I must have heard her say *chéri* about five times. Pretty sure that's French for *sweetheart.*"

The idea of Gigi having a sweetheart was chilling. She didn't exactly come across as the lovey-dovey type.

"Okay if I give Webster a treat?" Madz asked, holding up a small baggie of Cheerios. "I saw you feeding him some yesterday."

I nodded. "Sure. He loves those. Just a half at a time, though. He doesn't have teeth."

A moment later Gigi marched back into class, tossed the phone on her desk, and frowned at it for a few seconds. Then she turned to face us, clapping her hands in that way teachers do when they're trying to get you to settle down. Only *we* weren't the ones who'd been gabbing on our phones.

"Bonjour, children. Today, we return to our learning of French cuisine with another traditional but simple dish—" Her phone pinged and she glanced down at it briefly before continuing. "Zee croque monsieur! Page twenty-six in the recipe book, if you please."

There was a ruffle of paper as the three of us flipped the pages to find the recipe. Madz got there first.

"Really, dude?" she said with a snort. "It's a cheese sandwich."

I scanned the recipe to see if she was right.

Darn.

The one thing I already knew how to make.

I raised my hand to say something, but Gigi's attention was on her phone as it pinged again . . . and then again. She picked it up and stared at it for a minute, her red lipsticked mouth twisting into a grimace. Then with a huff, she hurled it into the top drawer of the desk and closed it with a bang. I'm no expert on romance, but I guessed she and her sweetheart were in the middle of a fight.

She spun around to face us, flashing her toothpaste-model smile like nothing was wrong. "As I was saying, in French cooking, we use only the most fresh ingredients." She strode to the fridge, pulled out a loaf of bread, and placed it on a cutting board.

Ping.

"First step is to slice the baguette." She gave it a sniff and a little squeeze. Her nose crinkled. "Ah, but this is no good," she mumbled under her breath.

Ping.

Ping.

"Do you need to answer that?" Madz said. "Because we can wait."

"*Non,*" she snapped, returning to the fridge. For a minute, all we could hear was shuffling packages and clinking jars. "But where is the cheese I requested?" I heard her groan. My eyes skipped over to Madz, who was patting her stomach with a very self-satisfied grin on her face.

Whoops.

Ping.

Gigi swung the fridge door shut and turned to face

us. "A moment please," she said, holding up a finger. She walked around her desk and pulled open her drawer. She was concentrating so intensely, you'd think she was trying to solve a geometry question. When she closed it again, she looked like she was trying not to cry. For a nanosecond, I actually felt sorry for her. I was about to ask if she was okay, but then she pulled her shoulders back and announced: "I think we will go to the market."

JD, Madz and I exchanged surprised glances. "The food market? Now?" JD asked. "Like, for a field trip?"

"Yes, yes. *Exactement.*"

"But don't you need permission to take us out of camp?"

"Pffft," she said with a flick of her hand.

"Ugh, don't we have any other cheese here?" Madz asked, not even a hint of guilt in her voice.

"Certainly. But not the one we require. And the other ingredients in this kitchen are not fresh enough! Look at this bread." She picked it up and brought it down hard against the cutting board. It made a loud cracking sound as it connected with the surface, like a dry branch breaking in half. She held it up for us to see. "Baked yesterday. Bah. Much too stale."

I stared at the mangled baguette in shock. I'd never seen anyone swing food around like a baseball bat before. This lady was something else. I had to admit, a tiny part of me liked the idea of escaping from this kitchen, even just for a short walk to the market. But the bigger, more rational part of me didn't want to go anywhere with wound-up Chef Gigi.

Ping.

She opened the lid of the compost bin and hurled the battered bread inside. "We will go immediately!"

Jeepers. What the heck did her "*chéri*" say that got her so riled?

I raised my hand. "Um, just saying, it's boiling hot out. And I didn't bring a sun hat."

"Yeah. And I don't remember seeing *physical activity* listed in the camp description," Madz added.

"It is not so far," Gigi replied, clucking her tongue and slamming the lid of the compost bin. "Come along!" She marched to the door, motioning for us to follow.

One by one, we peeled off our aprons and dropped them onto the island. Madz's black T-shirt of the day read *It's not me, it's you.*

"Give me a sec. I just have to get Webster ready," I said, pulling his leash out of my backpack.

"Ah, *non*! There is no time. We must go before all the fresh bread is sold," she said, tapping her foot impatiently. "The duck can stay here."

I couldn't believe she was trying to exclude Webster again. No way was I going to let that happen. "I *can't* leave him," I replied, looping him into his harness and fastening it around his back. "He'll get stressed in a strange place all by himself. And besides, who would keep him away from your food preparation areas?"

I stood up, hands on hips and ready to remind her about the rule she'd come up with herself. But luckily, Gigi seemed to be too preoccupied with whatever was going on with her *chéri* to argue.

Snake Skins and
Troll Dolls

With one last simmering glance over her shoulder, Gigi led us out of the classroom, down the hall, and out onto the sidewalk. The sun was shining brightly and the sky was clear. But there was no breeze and, unfortunately, it happened to be the hottest day of the summer so far. It was only ten in the morning, but I could practically feel the pavement scorching through the soles of my shoes. And it seemed to be getting hotter by the minute. Luckily I'd remembered to put Webster's shoes on today. They were good for keeping his feet from burning on a hot sidewalk.

Gigi led the way, back on her phone again and charging ahead like she was trying to escape from a zombie invasion. The three of us kids trailed behind her, and Webster trailed behind us, waddling on his leash and pecking occasionally at a bug or patch of grass. Less than a minute into our field trip, I was already sweating through my T-shirt and wishing I'd remembered to bring some water.

"So, I looked up that elephant last night," JD said. "Kids' books are cool."

I was surprised he'd remembered Babar's name. "Yeah. He's definitely a VIP."

"Sorry?"

"Very. Important. Pachyderm."

He smiled. "Is that Babar too?" he asked, pointing to my new necklace.

"No. This one's just a regular elephant." After a second I added. "I sort of collect them."

"Cool," Madz said, kicking a rock with her flip-flopped foot. "Why elephants?"

I told her what I tell everyone who asks that question. "Because they're good luck. And also 'cause they're from far away. You'd never find an elephant hanging around a place like the Spot. Amirite?"

"Totally," she said, popping one of Webster's left-over Cheerios into her mouth. "Fun fact: they're also the feminists of the animal world."

JD peered at her over the top of his glasses. "They're *whatnow*?"

"Feminists. The male elephants run away and live solo, while the female elephants rear the children, feed and protect the herd, make all the family decisions and support each other. Those girls do it all!"

I stared at her in amazement. "How do you know that?"

"I watch the nature channel a lot," she said with a shrug. "And I collect stuff too."

I wasn't completely sure I wanted to hear the answer, but I was too curious not to ask. "Really? Like what?"

She shuffled to the side and stomped on a large crack in the sidewalk. It seemed like she was going out of her way to get them all. "Snake skins. Mini hotel soaps. Back scratchers. Slime. But my best collection is my troll dolls. I have over a hundred."

"Oh, wow. Awesome," I replied. But I was really just trying hard to be nice. Snake skins and slime were cool. But troll dolls . . . really? Those things creeped me out. This girl was turning out to be weirder than Gran. At least her tiny spoon collection wasn't the stuff of nightmares. I fanned my T-shirt, trying to get some air on my sweaty skin. "Aren't you boiling in all those black clothes?" I added.

"Meh. I'm used to it."

Gigi was far ahead of us now. I tried to move Webster along, but he was walking slower than usual.

JD bumped me with his shoulder. "Hey, Mac?"

"Yes," I said, resigning myself to the nickname. It

could have been worse. At least he wasn't calling me Gnocchi Knees like Vicki Hoskins did in gymnastic camp last month. Or Spaghetti Legs like Robbie Vindereen did every day from September to April in grade five until our principal, Mr. Argentia, made him stop. In comparison, Mac wasn't really all that bad. And he smiled when he said it, so I knew he wasn't trying to be mean. "What is it?"

"*Penne* for your thoughts?"

I groaned, but decided not to dignify that one with an answer. "Come on, Webster," I said, tugging gently on his leash.

"Sorry . . . but the joke *pasta*bilities are endless," JD added, slapping his knee, clearly entertained by his own dumb humour.

I pursed my lips and walked faster. We were passing a lawn with one of those rapid-blasting fast-turning sprinklers. I imagined myself pushing him into it and smiled.

"I *cannelloni* do so much," he said, hurrying to catch up. "I'm *pasta* the point of no return!"

I stopped walking and whirled around to face him. I wasn't smiling anymore. The sun was burning my scalp, the sweaty cotton of my T-shirt was cemented uncomfortably to my back and I was fresh out of patience.

"Enough!" I snapped.

It was way too hot for stupid noodle jokes. To make matters worse, JD didn't seem bothered at all by the heat. In fact, he was grinning so hard, his lips had almost disappeared. I'd never noticed his dimples before. They were sort of adorable.

"Sorry, did I go *pasta* the line?" he cackled.

I gave him my best impression of an Oscar the Grouch glare. But it was hard to stay mad at a bunch of cheesy puns. Plus those dimples of his were wearing down my defences. "Stop! It! Now!" I said flicking his ear. "Not original!"

He held up his hands in surrender. "Okay, sorry, sorry. I'll stop now. For real."

"Finally," I said, feeling my frustration fading. I could see in his face that he meant it.

In her quest to trample all the sidewalk lines and cracks, Madz had fallen behind us a bit. But now she stomped her way over to where we were standing just in time to hear JD's apology.

"If I was you," she said, snapping her gum and nudging me with an elbow, "I wouldn't forgive him unless he tells us what that *D* stands for."

I thought it over for a few seconds. "That sounds fair."

JD stopped walking. "No way," he said, his grin disintegrating.

"Oh please. It can't be *that* bad."

"I could tell you. But then I'd have to kill you both."

"Dudley?" Madz guessed. "Dwayne?"

"I bet it's Dagwood?" I giggled, enjoying giving him a taste of his own medicine. "Oh, I know . . . Declan?"

"Diablo?"

"Donatello?"

"Donald?"

"Um . . . Derwin?"

"I got it! Dweezil?"

I shot Madz a look. "Really?"

JD waved off each one of our guesses. "Nice try, kids. But you'll never get it, so you should save yourself the effort."

"I'll tell you *my* middle name," Madz piped up. "It's Gertrude. I hate it. And there's no way yours could be worse than that."

"Sorry to hear about your middle name trauma, Trudy. But I'm still not telling you mine."

"Come on. I'll tell you mine too," I added. "Spoiler alert: it's *not* Macaroni."

Madz held out her hand for a high-five. "Solidarity, sister!"

"Tempting offer," he said walking ahead of us. "But I think I'll pass."

We were taking a shortcut through a residential part of town where it seemed like every other lawn had a sprinkler running. I was so hot that at this point, I was considering running through one myself.

"Hey, is Webster okay?" Madz asked, crouching down beside him. "It sounds like he's panting."

We had stopped walking so he could nibble at a patch of clover. Or so I thought. But when I looked down, I was surprised to see he wasn't eating. I knelt beside him for a closer look.

"You okay, Feather Butt?"

I ran my hands over his feathers. He didn't feel overly warm. But Madz was right. He *was* panting a bit, which was extremely worrisome. I wasn't a vet or anything, but I knew enough to understand that duck panting was not good. Maybe it wasn't such a smart idea to bring him along. I stood up and cupped a hand around my mouth. "Excuse me? Chef Gigi?" At this point, she was so far ahead of us, I had to yell. "Can we stop somewhere for some water? I'm worried my duck might be overheating."

She stopped walking abruptly and turned around. I could see her glare from a whole block away.

"Is this a joke?" she called back, lowering her phone.

"No," I yelled again. "Absolutely not a joke!"

I could sense her growing annoyance as she clicked off her phone and started marching back to where we had stopped. By the time she reached us, she looked like she was about to erupt into another one of her tantrums.

"Sorry, but it's really hot out here," I said. "I think he needs to cool off."

"I told you to leave the beast back in the kitchen," she said, staring down at Webster. She actually seemed concerned about him. "Will he drink Perrier? I maybe have one in my bag." She pulled open the straps and rifled through the contents. But when she looked up again, her expression had changed. Now she just looked seriously cheesed. "*Zut.* I have lost my wallet. I must go back. *Excusez-moi!*"

Without another word, she trotted off back in the direction of the community centre.

"But what about the fresh bread?" JD asked. "Don't we have to get there before it's all sold?"

"Keep walking!" she called over her shoulder. "I will meet you there!" A minute later, she turned a corner and was gone.

The four of us stared at each other in astonishment.

"Is she allowed to just leave like that?" I asked.

Madz shrugged and gathered Webster into her arms. "Just sayin' . . . this is legit the strangest camp I've ever been to."

Coming from her, I think that was meant to be a compliment.

Bad Omens

"So what do we do now?"

I looked around, trying to guesstimate how far we were from the market. Were we still going to the market? Poor Webster needed water immediately (or *subito* in Italian). Fresh bread didn't feel nearly so important anymore. Maybe it would be smarter to get him straight to the harbour for a swim.

"Hey, my house is right around that corner," JD said, pointing to a stop sign a few houses ahead. "We can go grab a drink for Webster and cool off there for a few minutes."

"Great . . . I could probably use some water too." My mouth was dry and I was starting to feel a bit light-headed. This heat was just too much.

When we got to his house, a woman in a pink sundress was leaning over a bed of red roses in the middle of a perfectly landscaped front yard. She tilted back her floppy hat and waved as we walked up the driveway. I knew right away where JD got his carrot-coloured hair.

"Joshua. What are you doing here?"

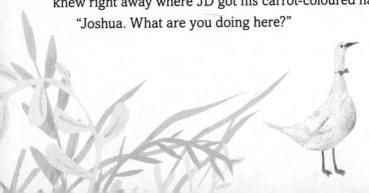

"We're out on a field trip."

"Really? To where?"

"The market. We're getting an on-site demonstration of the food selection process."

She pursed her lips and nodded, clearly impressed. "Well, that sounds very educational. Are these some of your camp friends?"

"Yep. Madz Schipper and Sarah Lasagna," he said, pointing us out. "And that's Webster. It's hot so we detoured for a drink."

She smiled and wiped a trickle of sweat off her forehead with the back of a gloved hand. "Nice to meet you, girls. And look at this little fellow. I've seen you walking with him around town. He's adorable."

"Thanks," I said, not surprised to hear that. Webster was kind of a local celebrity in the Spot.

"My goodness, you're tall, dear."

Yeesh. At this rate, I was well on my way to smashing a world record before my next birthday.

"And those lovely curls. You certainly *do* take after your father, don't you?"

What? I think my heart might have actually stopped. "Y-you knew my father?"

"Of course. I was there the day he and your mother met."

I wasn't expecting that. At all. "You were?" I gasped, blinking hard. This had to be a dream. Or maybe this heat was making me delirious.

"Didn't she ever tell you the story?" Mrs. Granger took a small step back so she was standing in a patch of shade and motioned for me to join her. Despite the scorching sun on my head, I stayed where I was because it seemed my feet were cemented to the driveway.

"Caroline and I were on break from our jobs," she explained. "The two of us were teaching evening classes at Miss Tina's dance studio. Your father was working on a private yacht that had been touring up and down the coast, and on this particular night they had dropped anchor right here in the Spot harbour. He was standing on the deck when he saw Caroline and me on the shore. He waved at her and I guess she must have waved back and that was it. He dove in the water right then and there, uniform and all. And just like that, he was swimming ashore and had her swept up in this big, romantic kiss. It was the most exciting thing anyone around here had ever seen. I tell you, if I wasn't already married, I would have swooped in there myself."

She thumped the spot on her chest just over her heart and closed her eyes, like she was remembering something from a dream. "Sorry to go on like that. I'm sure you've heard this a million times before."

I had heard some of it, yeah. Scraps of information from various people over the years. But the way she told it made me feel like I was watching one of those old romantic black-and-white movies. My head was spinning with images of Papa and Mombo falling in love. My pulse was pounding a wild drumbeat in my ears.

"He was so tall and she was so tiny. He was dark and she was so fair. They were startling in their differences." Mrs. Granger sighed and her eyes popped open again. "Who knows? Maybe that was a bad omen right from the get-go."

JD nudged her with his elbow. "Mom, don't!" I heard him whisper.

"No, it's okay," I said, holding up a hand to stop him. "Remind me — what happened next?" Nobody in my family ever shared stories about Papa. I was greedy for as much as I could get.

"Well, let's see . . . I believe he quit his job on the boat that very day and found a place to live here in the Spot. They were married less than a month later and you came along before the first year was up. And, well, I guess you know the rest."

She raised her eyebrows and smiled, like she expected me to pick up the story from there.

"Oh, yeah. Of course," I said, but I knew the words sounded forced and phony. I glanced down at my size tens, certain the truth was stamped across my face. And if I looked up now, they'd all know that I was a big old liar. Because the shameful truth was, I knew next to nothing about my own father. Not even his first name. I mean, what kind of daughter doesn't even know her own father's name? But when he left, I'd been too young to call him anything but Papa.

It crossed my mind that I could just ask Mrs. Granger what it was. She seemed like the type who liked to gossip. In fact, she was possibly a fountain of valuable information and more than likely not under orders from Mombo to keep any of it secret. I could get all the answers I needed for that search. But my pride stung at the idea of asking someone I'd just met to tell me about my own father. I'd probably die of mortification before I'd finish getting the words out.

"So, where is your father these days, dear?" she asked, cocking her head. "I don't think I ever did hear exactly where he ended up."

And, there it was. The thing every nosy person in the Spot wanted to know. The question that made the whispery rounds at parties and town picnics and Santa Claus parades. The mystery ending to the Spot's biggest scandal. Not for the first time, I found myself wishing I was smaller, because this would be a perfect time to just disappear into thin air. The sun beat down over my scalp as my brain tried to invent an answer to a completely different question.

hic

Mrs. Granger pressed on. "What's it been . . . ten years? Where's he living now? I've heard rumours he's on a mountain somewhere in South East Asia. How exotic! Do you hear from him at all?"

"Mom. Come on!" JD hissed.

"He's um, well . . . I think . . . *hic*." Tiny pinpricks of heat spread over my skin like a rash. I scratched weakly at my arms, looking for relief. Webster suddenly started pecking at my toes and clucking like he knew something was wrong. I tried to tell him I was fine. That it was just the heat and all I needed was a drink of water and for the nosy questions to go away. But my mouth was suddenly too dry to form words. I felt someone grabbing my arm.

"Dude, you okay?" Madz's voice sounded tinny and small, like it was coming from miles away. "You look like a ghost."

And then everything suddenly went dark.

Sizzling Bacon
in a Garden

The first thing I saw when I opened my eyes was Webster. He was perched on my stomach, beak pointed skyward, flapping his wings and quacking. Tiny white feathers floated in a cloud around us. Later that day, when I was able to think more clearly, I realized this must have been his way of trying to cool me off. My own personal wind machine.

Yeah, my baby's a genius.

The second thing I saw was JD's face hovering over mine. His glasses were off and his chocolate brown eyes were so wide with alarm, I could see my own face reflected in them. And there was a whole galaxy of rust-coloured freckles dotting his nose and cheeks.

"Are you okay?" he gasped.

I blinked a few times, trying to make sense of what was happening. Why was I lying on the grass? Why did my head feel like someone had whacked it with a wet pool noodle? And how had I not noticed all those freckles before? He leaned into my face, so close I could

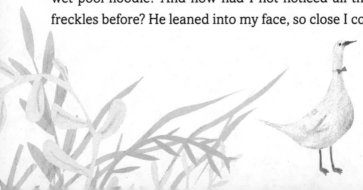

feel his breath on my skin. It smelled like mint chocolate chip ice cream. My favourite.

"I can't tell if your pupils are dilated," he said, peering into my eyes. "Can you speak?"

"Yeah. I . . . I'm fine."

"Are you sure? Do you know what year it is? Are you having difficulty breathing?"

"Move. I want to get up."

"I think maybe we should wait for—"

"I want to get up!"

Webster hopped to the side, quacking up a storm while JD put his glasses back on, took my hands, and helped me to my feet. "I'm sure you fainted," he said. "I've never seen anyone faint before. Although, of course, we covered it in my first aid course last summer. Luckily, my certificates are all up to date so if it happens again, I'll know what to do." He looked at me warily. "Do you feel like it might happen again?"

My knees wobbled as I tried to hold myself steady. My arms and legs felt like the bones had been sucked out of them.

"Whoa! I thought you were dying on us!" Madz said, grabbing my elbow to help keep me upright.

Mrs. Granger ran to hold the front door for us. Together, the three of them dragged me into the house and onto a wonderfully cool leather couch. Madz and JD sat on either side of me. Webster jumped onto my knees and laid his chin on my lap.

"I'm okay. Really." I said, resting my head on the back cushion. "Just give me a minute." I wasn't really sure who I was trying harder to convince — me or them. My head was still spinning and my stomach felt like it was trying to digest a bowl of molten lava.

JD pulled over an ottoman and shoved it under my feet. I could hear him muttering first aid notes under his breath. "Elevate the patient's legs . . ."

"It's probably just a touch of heat exhaustion, dear," Mrs. Granger said, fanning herself with a home decor magazine. "Totally understandable. For a minute, I felt hot like a strip of bacon sizzling in a pan standing out there in the garden."

For some reason, that just made my head feel even more dizzy. Was I suffering from a concussion? Or did that make absolutely no sense?

"Check for symptoms of dehydration," JD mumbled, grabbing my hand and pinching at the skin.

"Ouch!" I said, swatting him away.

"Dude. Give her some space," Madz growled.

"What's going on in here?"

I glanced up to see a red-haired girl standing in the

doorway with her hands on her hips. From the look on her freckled face, I could tell she was seriously cheesed.

"Nothing. Mind your own business, Carly," JD snapped.

"Pretty sure it *is* my business if someone's dying in my living room!"

"Chillax, kiddo," Madz cut in. "She's not dying. She just fainted."

"Well, why does she have to do it on our couch? That's where I sit when I — oh my gosh! Is that a *duck*?"

JD turned his attention back to his first aid checklist. "Don't mind my sister, Mac. It's not her fault she was born with a defective personality."

"Don't talk to me ever again," Carly sniffed, spinning around and stomping back off to wherever it was she came from.

"Oh, you kids. Just be nice," Mrs. Granger said, not even bothering to look up from her magazine. She'd stopped fanning herself a minute ago and was now thumbing through the articles.

"Water," I croaked. "I think maybe water would help."

"Oh, I know," Mrs. Granger said, dropping the magazine with a thunk on the glass coffee table. "Let me get you something to drink. Once you cool down, I'm sure you'll feel like yourself again."

"And the duck needs water too," Madz called out.

She came back a minute later with a glass of iced tea for me and a bowl of water for Webster, which she placed on the floor several feet away from the edge of her cream-coloured carpet. I sat up, put Webster down, and took a few tentative sips of the drink, worried it might come back up if I gulped it down the way I really wanted to. I'd already embarrassed myself enough today by fainting. I would probably die of acute mortification if I topped off the morning by hurling up tea on JD's living-room floor. Did I mention how his house was super-sparkling clean and smelled like bottled pine trees? Blah. I tried breathing through my mouth to keep it out, but it just found its way onto my tongue.

"Better now?" Mrs. Granger asked. "Do you want me to call your mother to come get you?"

I waved that idea away. "No, please don't bother. She wouldn't be able to leave the shop because of Helen's broken ankle and Doug and Shayna being away on vacation, but not together of course . . . and anyway, I'm feeling fine now. Almost a hundred percent."

I smiled, hoping to convince her (and myself) that it was true. The iced tea and air conditioning really seemed to be working miracles. At this point, as long as

Mrs. Granger didn't ask any more nosy questions about why Papa left, I'd be okay.

"If you're not in a hurry, maybe it would help even more if you went for a swim?" she suggested. "Our backyard's in the shade and our pool heater's off, so the water should be nice and cool. Although I'd hate for you to be late for that on-site demonstration at the market."

"Oh, that's not a problem. I'm sure they wouldn't start without us. And I agree, cool water immersion is a good suggestion — a very effective treatment for heat exhaustion," JD said. "We'll all go."

"Um, hello?" Madz scowled, "Lasagna and I don't have bathing suits, remember?"

"That's not a problem. Carly has a drawerful. You can borrow a couple of hers," Mrs Granger said, eyeing the two of us. "Although . . . she isn't quite as tall as you, dear," she added, her gaze flicking over the stretched-out dimensions of my giraffe-impersonating body. "But I think you'll be safe with one of her two-pieces."

"I'll take whatever. As long as it's black," Madz said, jumping to her feet.

While I didn't exactly love the idea of wearing another kid's bathing suit, the thought of going for a swim was too appealing to pass up. Not just for me, but for Webster too. I didn't have a chance to get him down to the harbour yet today. It would do him good to get into some water.

"That would be great. Thanks," I said, taking the last sip of my iced tea.

"Do you kids need me to come out there and supervise?" Mrs. Granger asked, pausing on her way to go find the bathing suits.

JD looked offended by that. "Mom. I've got my first aid training. Remember?"

"Oh yes. Very true."

"Plus, I'm twelve now," I added proudly. "So, like, officially legally independent in a swimming pool."

"That's quite a relief," Mrs. Granger said, with a smile.

Four pairs of eyes zoomed in on me as I rose to my feet. This time my knees co-operated.

We separated into different rooms to get changed. On my way into the powder room with my borrowed bikini, I noticed Mrs. Granger with a cleaning spray and cloth, wiping off the side of the couch where Webster and I had been sitting.

Yikes.

She and Gran would probably get along great.

Ripping Out Pages

Webster and I stepped out into the backyard just in time to see Madz cannonballing into the deep end, still dressed in her clothes. To her credit, at least she took off her shoes. I could only assume that meant Carly's bathing suit drawer didn't contain anything black or edgy enough to suit her taste.

JD cannonballed beside her and their collective splash sprayed water all over the deck, including the five pots of colourful flowers artfully placed around the edge of the pool. As soon as they came up for air, they each grabbed a water blaster. Madz managed to get the upper hand right from the get-go and in less than a minute, JD was backed into the corner beside the diving board, arms in the air and yelling for surrender.

I peeled off Webster's little shoes and waded into the pool slowly, hanging back on the bottom step and enjoying the feel of the cool water on my skin. I tried my best to keep him from going any farther than the top two steps. But it's not easy corralling a duck. Something told me Mrs. Granger wouldn't approve of him swimming in her pool— even though he still had his diaper on, so it's not like he'd make a mess.

"Hey, do you guys think Cheffy's waiting for us at the market?" Madz asked, tossing her blaster aside and reaching for an air mattress.

Looking relieved, JD lowered his arms and paddled out of shooting range before she could change her mind. "No. I think it's more likely she's still on her phone fighting with her *chéri.*"

"Maybe we should call the community centre to let her know what happened. You know . . . and tell her where we are," I said.

Madz looked at me like I'd lost my mind. "Are you in some kind of a hurry to go back and make cheese sandwiches?"

"No."

"Dude. Then drop it." She clung to the side of the air mattress for a minute. Her forehead was scrunched up like a rippled potato chip, which I can only assume was her "deep-thinking" face. "You guys ever wonder if clouds are real?" She tilted her face to the sky and squinted hard. "I have a theory that they're just cut and pasted up there."

I giggled, convinced she was pulling our legs. But her expression stayed serious. "Um, really?" I coughed.

"Yup. And I have another theory that the moon isn't real. I believe it's all an elaborate 3-D projection."

JD shook his head sadly. "Congratulations. You just won the prize for the most far-fetched theories in the history of the universe."

She turned her gaze over to him. "Truth is stranger than fiction, bro. That's a scientific fact."

"Uh, no, it's not."

"Okay Mr. Smart Guy, how about *this* theory: I think Cheffy's a straight-up, Grade A, French phony."

Luckily, I managed to swallow my laughter this time. She still scared me a bit. I didn't want to get on her bad side. "That's, well, kind of . . . silly."

"Is it? Tell me, why would a fancy French chef come all the way from Paris to teach a kids' camp in a hick town like the Spot?"

"I don't know. Money probably. Maybe they offered her a pile of it?"

"Maybe . . . but not likely. It's gotta be something else. Like, maybe she's hiding out from the law. Or maybe she's been placed in a witness protection program and this is her cover."

I shook my head. "Why are you so suspicious?"

"Um, because I have eyes?" she said, blinking them dramatically, just in case we weren't sure what that meant. "I just can't picture this crummy town paying anyone big bucks. For anything. Something about it just doesn't make sense."

"Not everything's a conspiracy." I leaned back on my elbows and let my legs float out in front of me. "What made you two sign up for this stupid camp anyway?"

JD looked like he was about to answer, but stopped. "Do you really want to know?" he finally said, scooping a stray leaf out of the pool.

"Yeah. Wait. No. It's not something really sad, is it? Like homeless puppies?"

"No, nothing like that." He picked up a beach ball and tossed it at me. "It's just . . . Aw, you're going to laugh."

"I won't."

"Promise?"

I nodded and held up my hand like I was taking a vow.

"Okay, well. I didn't like how the culinary arts section of my resumé was blank. I sort of wanted something to fill it with." The tips of his ears were already pink from the sun. But with every word of this confession, they turned brighter and brighter. If we could switch off the daylight for a minute, I'd bet a month of allowance they'd glow in the dark.

Madz snorted loud enough to make a rhinoceros mama proud. "Seriously?" she asked, clutching the edge of the mattress like she was going to fall off.

"See?" JD said, slapping the water in frustration. "I knew you'd laugh."

"Sarah promised. Not me."

"You gotta admit," I said, "it does sort of sound like a joke."

His face went deadly serious. "I never, ever joke about my resumé."

Was this guy for real? "You think *this* cooking camp is going to help you get a job?"

"One day, maybe. Employers like well-rounded candidates. And I've been told we get a certificate at the end of the week."

"But you're just a kid. Who's going to hire you?"

"I like to be prepared for every possibility. My parents have high . . . *expectations* for me. And Carly too, of course. But she's the baby so they focus most of their intensity on me."

I thought about that for a minute. The way he said *expectations* made it sound like a code word for something else. Something not altogether good.

"How about you, Madz?" I asked, tossing her the beach ball. She ignored it and it sailed right over her head and landed with a plop under the diving board. "Why are you here?"

"My parents really wanted me to go to a wilderness retreat camp this summer," she said, grunting as she hauled herself on to a kissy-face emoji air mattress. Her pigtails were dripping and her wet clothes were plastered to her like a second skin. "Like, my mom went to one the summer she was going into grade seven and she said it was the best thing that ever happened to her. So one day in June they brought home a bunch of brochures and left them on my bed."

Well, that sounded like the answer to a completely different question. Which is totally a page out of my playbook. Did that mean we were being too nosy? I waited for her to get to the part that made sense. But she seemed more interested in flopping out on her back like a human starfish.

"Am I missing something?" JD asked. "If you signed up for a wilderness retreat, how on earth did you wind up at cooking camp?"

She tilted her chin to the sky and closed her eyes. "Because I dumped their dumb wilderness retreat brochures into the recycling bin. That's why."

Holy crust. Following her logic was turning out to be harder than learning Italian.

"Okay, wait . . . can you rewind a bit? I still don't understand."

Madz sat up on an elbow and rolled her eyes so hard I wouldn't be surprised if she got a peek at her own brain. "Listen up, yo-yos. Ever since my parents forced us to move here, I've had this thing where I do the *opposite* of whatever it is they want me to do. It's how I've been dealing with my anger — at them, at my teachers, at this whole stupid town. Get it? So when they started pushing a wilderness retreat camp, I naturally searched up camps that were as completely different as possible and signed myself right up. Lego camp. Book camp. Tap dance camp . . . that one was actually kinda fun. My parents weren't happy at all. Which, of course, was exactly the point." She tapped the side of her head like she was a genius.

Huh. Maybe in an alternate-universe sort of way, she was.

"Ah, okay. I guess that kinda makes sense," I said, surprised but not entirely shocked that the same girl who would wear a *Hangry* T-shirt and army boots to the grade six dance would sacrifice her summer plans to get revenge on her parents.

"Huh. Spite camp," JD said, sounding impressed. "How very revolutionary,"

She leaned back on the mattress and closed her eyes again. "My dudes! Forget colouring outside the lines," she said, snapping her fingers. "Sometimes you just have to rip out the whole page!"

There was a loud, high-pitched gasp from behind and we all turned at once to see where it came from. Carly was back, standing in front of the open doorway and pointing a skinny, freckled finger right at Webster.

"Oh. My. God. Is that duck allowed to be in our *pool*?"

JD groaned. "It's fine, okay? He's wearing a diaper."

Poor Carly looked like she'd just been handed a plate of vomit. Her face was so green, it was almost funny. "Ew. That is just *so* gross, I can't even."

"Then don't even," JD snarled. "Just go away and leave us alone!"

She stomped her flip-flopped foot. "This is my backyard too, you know!"

Clearly, Madz wasn't the only one dealing with anger issues. Seems to me Carly could use an emotionally supportive pet of her own.

"Are you even listening to me?" she screeched.

One look at Madz's face and I knew she'd had enough. In a sequence of rapid, coordinated moves, she'd loaded up her blaster and was shooting a perfectly aimed stream of water at Carly's curly red head before she could utter another bratty word. Carly shrieked and darted back into the house. "Mom!" I heard her yelling, "That icky duck is in our pool!"

I reached out and gathered Webster into my arms. He nibbled on the ends of my hair, which I'm pretty sure meant *I love you*. He must have sensed I was feeling emotionally needy. "Well, at least you two had choices."

"This camp wasn't your choice?" Madz asked.

I shook my head and lowered my face into Webster's feathers. "I'm only here because my mother had nowhere else for me to go."

Maybe that came out sounding more pathetic than I intended, because a moment later JD swam over and took a seat beside me on the steps. Oh no. Was that pity in his eyes?

"I'm really sorry my mom asked about your father. I could tell that bugged you. It was really none of her business."

I wasn't sure what to say. Should I tell him how I die a bit inside every time someone asks where Papa is? How I wake up every day feeling perfectly normal until the moment when someone inevitably looks at me or Mombo a certain way at a grocery store or a movie theatre, or we walk past other families — complete, happy, smiling families — and for a flash of a second I see us the way they're seeing us. Abandoned. Unwanted. Broken. And it hits me like a punch in the heart every single time. The looks of sympathy are bad enough. But the worst is when they start asking questions — questions I'll probably never know the answers to. And how that always makes me want to run home, crawl into my bed, and hide under my blanket with Webster for the rest of my life.

Yeah, I know, lots of kids have parents who split up. But *I* am the kid with the father who left without a good-bye. The father who never came back for weekends or holiday visits. The one who didn't care enough to send even one measly postcard in ten years.

Should I tell JD how I feel like the first thing people see when they look at me is the giant piece that's missing?

It was too much to put into words. So in the end, I just held Webster even tighter. And didn't say anything at all.

Dear Papa,

Today I heard a story about how you and Mombo met. It sounded like you two were in love. I wish I had memories of the three of us together.

Mombo doesn't dance anymore. She doesn't sing either.

Not since you went away.

I thought you should know.

If it was something I did, I'm really, really sorry.

I'd like to come visit you, wherever you are.

Where are you?

Your daughter,

Sarah

P.S. Just wondering, how old were you when you stopped growing?

Last Night

Webster slept beside me on my pillow, nose to beak. The soft warmth and nearness of him helped to slow my racing thoughts and calm my nerves after the stress of the day.

"Love you, Feather Butt," I whispered. Then I ran my fingers over his smooth back, closed my eyes and matched my breaths to his, or maybe he matched his to mine, and after a few minutes we had fallen into a sweet, slow, perfect rhythm.

Like a pair of synchronized sleepers playing a lullaby nobody else was allowed to hear.

It Goes Like This

In my imagination, my reunion with Papa goes like this.

It's spring and the sun is shining. I'll be walking home from school, minding my own business, and when I turn the corner onto our street he'll be standing right there in the middle of the sidewalk, waiting for me. And even though he won't have seen me since I was two-and-a-half years old and much, much shorter, he'll somehow know it's me and he'll hold out his suntanned arms.

"There's my daughter, Sarah!" he'll boom, walking toward me and smiling. Everyone on the street will stop what they're doing and turn to watch. And when he gets closer, I'll see the tears sparkling behind his glasses. "I am so sorry I left you," he'll say. "But I am here now. And your mother has invited me to come live with you again. I will be your father and we will make up for all the years we have missed."

And then I'll run into his arms, and he'll lift me off my feet and twirl me around.

"Leaving you was the biggest mistake of my life.

Please, please, please forgive me," he'll beg.

And I'll tell him I will. And make him promise to never, ever leave again.

And he'll promise.

Everyone on the street will break into applause.

And then I'll take Papa's hand and lead him upstairs and introduce him to Webster.

The Great Omelette Kerfuffle

"You look very handsome," I told Webster, smoothing down his feathers and straightening his tie. He cooed happily and nuzzled his chin on my shoulder. "Watch and see. That French snob will regret the day she called you a beast. Amirite?"

I figured the time had come to end this feud between Gigi and Webster. So this morning, I'd dug up his old ring bearer tie and fastened it around his neck after drying him off from his morning swim.

"Say cheese," I said, snapping a quick photo of us on my phone. Show me a person who can resist a duck in a pink bow tie, and I'll show you a person with a shrivelled-up black banana for a soul.

"Okay, let's do this." I gave Webster a quick kiss on the head and pushed open the door to room 113.

I knew something was off the second we stepped inside.

Webster and I were the last to arrive today. But instead of being greeted by JD's dumb jokes or Madz's

scowl or Gigi's chattering voice and pinging phone, there was just awkward silence.

I paused in surprise, scanning the kitchen for the culprit. And since it wasn't a huge space, I found it pretty quickly. Mombo's cousin, Jerry, was seated behind the desk, hands clasped neatly in front of him. He gave me a quick wave as I passed by.

Jerry is older than Mombo by about fifteen years. He has bushy eyebrows and a shiny bald head. He was wearing a pair of large dark-framed glasses and a no-nonsense frown. You could tell he was a Cameron from those signature family ears — slightly pointed on top, like an elf or a gnome. Grandad has them. Mombo too (but at least hers are hidden under her hair). I must have gotten my ears from Papa. #phew

Gigi was standing to the side, nervously tapping a sandalled toe and chewing on her thumbnail. *Yikes.* Could this have anything to do with our disaster of a "field trip?"

Apparently, yesterday while we were outside swimming, Mrs. Granger had decided to call the community centre and explain what happened and why we were cooling off at her house. I'm guessing she also might have shared some critical thoughts about the failed field trip and lack of supervision. She seems like the type who likes to complain. But by the time Gigi finally came back to meet us at JD's house, she seemed way more upset about missing out on the day's fresh bread than she did about my fainting spell.

She frogmarched us back to camp just in time for pick-up. The croque monsieur lesson was dead and buried before it ever took its first breath.

So, was Gigi in trouble now? Was Jerry here to take over the camp? I wasn't so sure how I felt about that. Gigi wasn't the best instructor. But at least she was entertaining. Jerry was a nice guy and all, but painfully dull. I'd rather watch a snail marathon than have to spend eight hours in a kitchen with him.

"Hello, little one. How are you today?" she said, blowing Webster a kiss as we passed by her desk. "Such a nice duck." She reached into her purse and pulled out a small paper bag. "Here," she said, handing it to me. "I brought him a treat."

Huh? I glanced around, wondering if this was a joke. JD's eyebrows flew up and he shot me a glance that screamed: *The heck?* Madz looked like she'd just seen a dead fish. I noticed her angry black T-shirt of the day read *Not Your Puppet*.

I peeked inside the bag, not sure what to expect. Duck poison? Dirt? Rocks? Instead, I found a generous scoop of fresh corn niblets. Webster loves them!

"Oh. Uh . . . thanks," I mumbled. Why was she suddenly being so nice?

Was the bow tie working its adorable magic already? Or was she just pretending to be a Webster fan to make up for yesterday's disastrous attempt at a cooking lesson?

Something sure didn't smell right. And it wasn't the perma-linger of burnt cheese. I'd accidentally dropped my elephant necklace in the toilet this morning. And I'd forgotten to turn around seven times after drop-off. I just hoped this didn't mean bad luck was coming for me.

I settled Webster in his usual spot by the window and gave him a few pieces of corn before joining the others at the counter.

"Children, you see we have a guest this morning," Gigi announced with a big, toothy grin. "Monsieur Cameron will be observing our cooking lesson. And perhaps he will even stay and join us for some eating too, eh? Wouldn't it be nice to have a guest at our table?"

Madz rolled her eyes. "Ish."

There was something phony about Gigi's smile today. It was so wide and open I worried her face might actually crack in half.

For the first time, I found myself wondering if Madz

might actually be on to something with her bizzare conspiracy theories.

"And now we move up to the next stage of cooking," she went on. "This recipe has a very much higher level of difficulty, but I believe you are ready."

Ready? How? We hadn't made one edible thing yet.

She clapped her hands, glanced over her shoulder, and batted her false eyelashes at Jerry. "This dish is one of my most favourites. Today we will master the art of the classic French omelette! Exciting, yes? We begin with—"

She stopped mid-sentence as a loud clatter tore through the room. It sounded exactly how I'd imagine an explosive robot fart would sound. If robots had digestive systems. It took me a moment to figure out it was coming from the air vent on the ceiling over Gigi's desk. A second later, there was a *clunk* followed by a stream of thick, smelly smoke wafting down from the vent.

Webster let out a squawk. I glanced over to see him pacing in small circles around his blanket. Poor baby. He is sensitive to loud noises and bad smells.

I held up my hand. "Excuse me? Can I take a moment to comfort my duck?"

"*Non!*" Gigi snapped. Her eyes were focused on the

long plume of smoke that was still streaming out of the wall. "That," she said, pointing to the vent, "does not look good."

"No, it doesn't," Cousin Jerry said, jumping to his feet. His giant forehead was furrowed in alarm. "Excuse me, please," he said, striding toward the door. "I'll be right back."

Gigi was clearly relieved to see him gone. "Listen, Monsieur Cameron is here to assess this camp and my skills as an instructor of the cooking," she said in a hushed voice, glancing over her shoulder like she was afraid he might come back before she could finish explaining. "So if you please, be on your best behaviour. Eh?" She turned to look at me. "No more fainting. Okay, yes? And no disturbance from—" she pointed over at Webster and sniffed "—the feathered beast."

Again? Every time she insulted Webster, it felt like a slap. "Please don't call him names," I insisted, fanning the air in front of my nose to keep the fumes away. "He's very sensitive."

"Come on. He's a duck. And what on earth is that silly thing on his neck?"

"It's a bow tie," I said tersely. "And I think he looks handsome."

Now there was a prickly, itchy heat spreading over

my chest. Was it getting hot in here already? Was the smoke irritating my skin? Or was I just stress-rashing? I fanned myself with both hands, hoping some airflow would help. Webster must have sensed my distress. Or maybe he felt the chilling darkness in Gigi's shrivelled black banana soul, because a second later he did something I've never seen him do before. Hopping off his blanket, he waddled over to where we were all standing.

"Websie-Woo?" I asked, walking over to meet him. "You okay?"

Ignoring me, he spread his wings, craned his neck, and stuck his tongue out at Gigi. A menacing hiss flew from his beak.

"Ack!" she cried, jumping in surprise.

"Webster!" I gasped. But I didn't exactly tell him to stop. I think any other duck mom would probably scold her baby for being so rude. But as far as I was concerned, Gigi had it coming. She'd pushed him too far with her insults.

She took a cautious step back. "Control your animal, if you please," she cried. "Or I will have it removed from my kitchen! We must all do our best to impress Monsieur Cameron today."

Madz held up a finger. "Why exactly are you so worried about impressing a small-town community centre director? Isn't Paris, like, the big time for you foodie people?"

Before she could answer, another loud clunk flew out of the air vent, followed by a metallic rattling and a booming thump. After that, there was an eerie silence as the smoke stream tapered off to a wisp. Gigi opened the door a crack and peeked out into the hall.

"Okay, no more questions!" she barked. "I think he is coming back now." She snapped her fingers. "Everybody in your places!"

"What places?" I glanced around to see if Madz or JD knew what she was talking about. But they looked just as confused as me. "You're making it sound like we're putting on a show here."

"I don't remember seeing the word *performance* listed in the camp description," Madz snorted.

"Yeah, sorry," JD said with a laugh, "but I'm not supposed to be performing without my agent present."

A hint of a smile tugged at Gigi's lips. Her hands quickly flew up to cover her mouth, but I'm almost certain I heard a giggle slip out. "Enough. Okay? Just stand there and be good!"

The three of us reluctantly tied on our aprons while Gigi went to the fridge to gather the ingredients for today's lesson. After yesterday's fiasco, I had my fingers crossed we wouldn't have to witness another baguette beating.

When Cousin Jerry returned to the kitchen a minute later, his face looked even more grim than before. If that was possible. "Bad news, I'm afraid," he said, lifting his glasses and scratching at his bushy brows. "The air conditioning's fan just died. The whole building's out."

A collective groan rolled through the room as we mourned yet another casualty of this horrible heat wave. According to Mombo, the heat wasn't going to be releasing its grip on our town for a few more days yet. In the meantime, it was leaving a path of blown-out machinery in its wake. This was turning into a really good week to be in the air conditioning repair business.

"Don't worry, people. Someone in maintenance is bringing up a fan right now. You'll all be fine until we get the system fixed and running again. For the time being though, we should open some windows."

"Brilliant. So, we can let *more* of the heat wave in?" Madz snorted.

"Actually, Ms. Schipper, it's so that we can let some of this toxic smoke out."

As Cousin Jerry went around opening windows, Gigi pasted her dazzling smile back on and resumed her cooking lesson. "Our recipe today is on page nineteen," she said, her voice dripping with honey. "We begin with the eggs. Grandmère Leblanc always said cracking an egg predicts fortune for the omelette. Be timid and weak when you crack the shell, your omelette will crumble. Crack with confidence, and your omelette will have success."

One by one, she brought the eggs down hard against the rim of the bowl. "You see? Like this."

A clucking sound was coming from the back of the room. I turned to see Webster pacing in circles, ruffling his feathers in agitation. And every time Gigi cracked an egg, he seemed to get worse. I caught his gaze and held a finger up to my lips. "Settle down," I mouthed silently.

"Mademoiselle Lasagna? If you please? Come try." She handed me a bowl and three eggs.

"Uh, I don't think that's a good idea," I said, glancing at Webster. Mombo and I try to be sensitive about cracking eggs around him.

"It is not hard. Come."

I held the egg in both hands and tapped it tentatively against the side of the bowl. I didn't want to rile Webster up any more than he already was. He really seemed to be having a problem with all this egg execution.

"*Non!*" Gigi said, "You must do it harder!"

I tried again with another egg, this time more like

the way she wanted. But I was too distracted by Webster to get it right. His pacing had escalated to stomping and I could hear him grunting and squeaking from all the way across the room. Between the farting air conditioner, Gigi's insults and her egg terrorism, his stress was getting worse by the minute. His hackles were up and he was giving Gigi a major stink-eye.

"Stop it," I mouthed, shaking my head at him. My eyes swept around the room. *Was anyone else noticing this?*

"*Non, non.* Like *zis!*" Gigi yelped, grabbing my hand and slamming the egg down on the rim with an ear-splitting *crack*. The shell split completely in two as the insides slipped out into the bowl. She smiled proudly, like she'd just pulled off a fancy card trick. "Bravo! You have success! Now again! Three eggs each omelette. Everyone, do it now."

She picked up a third egg put it into my hand and cracked it hard into the bowl. "*Voilà!*" she cried triumphantly.

I guess that final smashed egg was the straw that broke the duck's back because with a loud honk, Webster came running at Gigi, raising his wings and flapping like he was trying to take flight. He hopped on the counter, flapping and hooting and stomping so hard, he overturned my bowl of eggs and spilled them every-where.

Gigi shrieked and flew under the desk, covering her head like she was afraid he was going to peck off her hair. He followed close behind, hopping over to her desk and ducking his head under to where she was hiding. She screamed as he stuck out his tongue and hissed in her face.

"This animal is dangerous! Get him away from me! Now!"

By the time I finally managed to catch him and pull him away from Gigi, it was too late. There were feathers flying all over the place. Footprints in the butter. Eggs dripping down the counter and onto the floor. And a trail of broken dishes.

Cousin Jerry's no-nonsense frown grew so big, it took over his entire face. "I apologize, Sarah," he said. "I know we gave you permission for Webster to be in attendance here. But he's disrupting the class. Not to mention violating every health code in the book. I'll have to meet with the directors and figure out how to proceed from here, in a way that will respect and pro-tect the rights of everyone concerned. But in the mean-time, he can't stay in this kitchen."

"But he—"

"He'll have to wait outside in the hall until your mother can come pick him up."

I could feel a flood of tears building up in my eyes. "But she can't—"

He held up a hand to silence me. "I'm sorry, Sarah. But my decision is final."

Worse than Mucous Shoes

Looking back, I can only remember three things about that stupid omelette lesson. All of them terrible.

1. I felt lost without Webster in the room and my stomach was turning a sickening stress swirl the entire time.

2. I was so badly distracted by my stress, I spilled a bowl of raw eggs all over my apron, and the whites dripped down my legs and into my sneakers, and I wasn't wearing socks so it felt like I was walking in a squishy mucous puddle until eventually the eggs dried on my skin and started to smell and itch, which was possibly even worse.

3. Every omelette I tried to cook came out burnt or crumbled.

And in the end, not one of those terrible things mattered one bit. Because as soon as the lesson was over, the worst thing possible exploded like a nuclear-powered septic tank all over my life.

There weren't enough lucky elephants in the world to make it better.

Gone

I'll probably never know the exact details of what happened or why.

All I know is when I went out to the hallway to check on Webster . . .

. . . he was gone.

Duck, Duck, Loose

My desperate, throat-ripping, blood-curdling scream of terror brought them all running out into the hall.

"What happened?"

"Are you okay?"

"Where's Webster?"

"Ohmygodohmygodohmygodohmygodohmy-godohmygod," I shrieked, collapsing into a puddle on the floor. "HE'S GONE!"

Everyone spoke at once.

"What are you talking about?"

"Dude, relax! He's gotta be here somewhere."

"Are you telling me there's an unsupervised duck loose in this building?"

"Stand back. Give her breathing room. Do her pupils look dilated to you?"

"You see? I knew it. This duck is trouble."

"I'd just like to take a moment to remind everyone here that the community centre is not liable for mis-placed objects. Or pets."

"He's probably just wandering around or something.

You stuck him in an empty hallway. I wouldn't blame him if he got bored."

"*Excusez-moi* . . . but how do you think a duck can get bored?"

"Is she gonna faint again? Maybe we should get ready to catch her?"

"Has anyone checked the bathrooms?"

"*Mon Dieu* . . . now you think a bird could open a bathroom door?"

"Look at me, Mac . . . please."

But I couldn't look at him. I couldn't look at any of them. My eyes were super-glued to the window at the end of the hall. One of the windows Cousin Jerry had opened to air out the stinking air conditioning fumes. I raised a trembling hand and pointed at what was under the ledge.

A single, tiny white feather.

Search Party

JD sprang over to the window and poked his head out. When he turned around again, his face was scrunched with worry.

"Can Webster fly?"

I shook my head. "Not that I know of."

"Well, we're only on the first floor. He could have just hopped down to the ground. Let's split up and start searching."

"Good idea," said Cousin Jerry. "I'll go through the building, room by room. Just in case. Maybe somebody moved him."

Gigi sighed. "I suppose I can check the parking lot."

Madz grabbed my hands and pulled me to my feet. "I've got my bike here," she said. "Do you want me to see if maybe he went to your house? Are ducks like homing pigeons that way?"

"I don't know . . . I don't know," I wailed, pacing around in a rough, jerky circle. My feet suddenly needed to move, but I didn't know where. "Oh, gosh! Should we *hic* call the police? Maybe they can put up some roadblocks? Or send *hic* out an alert?"

"Pfft. A roadblock for a duck?"

JD put a steadying hand on my shoulder. "Keep calm, Mac. It'll be okay. We'll help you look for him."

I *so* wanted to keep calm. More than anything, I wanted to take Grandad's advice and be like a duck. Calm meant there was nothing to be afraid of. Calm meant everything in life was going okay. Calm meant I was in control of the situation. Calm meant I was paddling steadily toward a destination. Too bad calm was the absolute complete and utter opposite of what I was feeling in that moment. Sheer panic had taken hold of my body. My heart was lodged in my throat, my breath was coming out in short gasps, and my mind was racing with questions. I was a massive human stress spiral.

Fact is, I had no idea how to be like a duck without my pet duck beside me.

"I don't know . . . I don't know where he would go," I said, the words tumbling over each other on their way out of my mouth. "He's never done anything like this before!" I started pacing even faster. I had so much adrenaline pumping through me, I felt like I was going to pop out of my own skin.

Beside me, Gigi made a clucking sound with her tongue. "There is a first time for everything, eh?"

My whole life, I don't think I'd ever actually been tempted to smack another person until that moment.

"Oh no! What if someone stole him!" I wailed.

"*Mon Dieu,*" Gigi rolled her eyes. "'Who would steal a duck?"

"I don't know! All I know is that he hates *hic* being apart from me. And, oh gosh, it's even hotter out there than *hic* yesterday." I turned and started sprinting down the hall. I had to get out of this building and start looking for him. "What if he starts panting again? He's going to need water and—"

I stopped in my tracks as the words left my mouth. *Of course! That's it!* I took a deep breath, feeling my chest unclenching slightly as I allowed myself to cling to that possibility. It made so much sense. It had to be right.

"The harbour," I yelled. "He must have gone there to cool off. He's probably swimming right now. I gotta go bring him back!"

I spun around and flew down the hallway toward the main entrance.

Mombo. I need her to come meet me, I thought, fumbling in my pocket for my phone and punching my speed-dial entry for her cell. But she must not have activated the voicemail on her new phone because it just rang and rang. "Come on . . . answer!" I yelled at the screen as I careened out the front door of the centre. I clicked off and tried again, but still no luck.

I paused for a second in the parking lot to catch my breath and tap out a text.

help me. webster's missing

"Are we walking? Or do you have a lift?" a voice beside me asked. I jumped and whipped my head around. JD was standing right beside me. How long had he been there?

"Walking? Why? What are you—"

"I'm coming with you."

"No. Really, *hic* I don't need—"

"I know what you're going to say. Okay? But I don't care. I'm coming. You shouldn't be alone right now."

There was no time to argue. "Fine. Just don't hold me *hic* back. And NO pasta jokes!"

"Deal." He tucked his phone into his pocket. "Let's go."

It was way too sweltering to run. But I did it anyway, at top speed, all the way to the harbour. With poor JD at my heels, panting and huffing and puffing but never once cracking a joke or asking me to slow down. By the time we got there, we were both so utterly drenched in sweat it looked like we'd just got caught in a rainstorm.

And JD was so completely out of breath, it was ridiculous.

"Hey . . . you . . . ever . . . wondered . . . why they . . . call it . . . a . . . search party?" he panted, doubling over like he was trying to work out a running cramp. "It's not like . . . losing something . . . is a good time to celebrate. Unless you're serving . . . chips and dip . . . while everybody searches?"

I knew he was trying to be helpful and distract me from my panic. But I wasn't in the mood for his cheesy humour. "Do you see him?" I asked, scanning the shoreline for Webster. I'd been so sure I'd find him right here paddling around in the shallows, and he'd see me and run right over and everything would be okay again.

"Web-ster? Where are you, Waddle-Bunny?" I shrieked, cupping my hands around my mouth like a foghorn. "Web-sterrrrrrr!"

But he didn't come and I couldn't see him anywhere. To my surprise, however, I did see Gran. There she was, strolling down the boardwalk, wearing a blue muumuu and a big floppy straw hat, and leading Lola on her leash. I sprinted over to catch up with her, which wasn't hard because she was moving at a shuffling grandma pace. Her hat was so big, she didn't see me coming.

"Oh, dear me!" she yelped, clutching her chest.

"What in heaven's name are you doing sneaking up on a senior citizen like that?"

"Sorry, Gran! I—"

"And why on earth are you dripping? Did you go swimming in your clothes? Honestly, young people today are so vulgar."

"No . . . it's just . . . I'm *hic* just in a huge hurry to find Webster. He's lost. You haven't seen him around here, have you?"

Gran's irritated scowl softened into concern.

"No, dear. I haven't seen your duck." She raised a hand over her eyes and glanced around the harbour. "How long has it been missing?"

"He. He's a *he*, Gran. And for about an hour . . . and . . . and . . . it's too hot for him *hic* out here," I sniffed, feeling the prickle of hot tears building up behind my eyes. "And what if he's scared and stressing without me? Or what if he's been ducknapped and *hic* they're not treating him well? And I can't reach Mombo and I—" It hurt to talk. The words were scraping my throat raw.

Gran took my hands in hers and squeezed them tight. I had no idea her grip was this strong. "I will help you," she said, in a voice so beautifully low and calm it was like cool water over a sunburn. "We will find your duck. Don't you worry."

Maybe it's because this was the first time she'd ever shown concern for Webster. Or maybe it was because these were the exact words I'd needed so badly to hear. But as soon as she said them, I felt a bit better.

"Now I really must get out of this heat. Come up to the house with me and we'll dry you off and work out a plan. I'll call your mother at work and let her know what's happened. We'll have that duck of yours back by nightfall."

She turned around and started leading me in the direction of the beach house. "But wait," I said, holding back nervously, "what about Grandad? This would probably disturb his peace and quiet."

"These are extreme circumstances. And besides, he's been bored out of his mind all week. He'll be thrilled for a distraction."

I leaned down and gave her a hug. I really didn't know if this sudden show of concern was for me or Webster or both. But I guess it didn't matter. I was just so grateful for it. "Can someone from camp come with us?" I looked over my shoulder and spotted JD standing a few metres behind me, looking at something on his phone. I waved him over.

"This is my grandmother, Lillian Cameron. And that's Lola the pug."

He reached out to shake her hand, like the budding politician he was. "JD Granger. Nice to meet you. I go to camp with your granddaughter."

"Oh yes. You must be Paulette and Neil's boy?"

"That's right, ma'am."

Gran nodded. "Your mother took over as chairwoman of the BBTS Ladies' Auxiliary after I left. From what I've heard, she's doing a . . . decent job." She skimmed a critical eye over his sweat-soaked clothes. "And did you go for a swim too?"

JD opened his mouth to reply, but nothing came out except a stupefied, squeaky *no*. Holy cow, the head of the debate team, and the dance and yearbook committees, president of our school's young politicians club, and incoming student council vice president was smacked speechless by my Gran.

She had such a way with people.

"Well, you're welcome to join our little search party," she went on. "Good thing I went to the market earlier today. Do you kids like chips and dip?"

Well of course that gave me a giggle. And once I started, I couldn't make myself stop. JD joined in after a second, and Gran looked at us like we'd lost our minds, which just made us laugh even harder. It felt good. I could feel the awful panic in my chest ease a bit.

Huh. Maybe JD's humour wasn't as completely useless as I'd thought.

Gran didn't have a lot of patience for silliness. She turned around and started shuffling back toward the beach house, yelling at me to follow.

"So, are you coming with?" I asked, gesturing for him to join us.

He glanced down at his phone again. "You two go ahead for now. I'll catch up with Madz and see if she's had any luck yet. We'll meet you there."

"Okay. It's that house," I said, pointing up the shoreline. "You see it? The big one on the end of the point."

"Yeah, got it. I'll see you soon."

Grandma Style

No luck yet :(On r way 2 u now
K cu soon

I pocketed my phone and glanced up to see Gran watching me, hand on her hip and a disapproving scrunch squatting between her eyebrows.

"Tsk tsk. Addicted already?" she asked, pushing open the front door. "The moment I saw that gadget, I just knew it was going to be trouble."

I wiped my sweaty bangs away from my forehead and sighed. "I was only reading a text from JD, Gran. Not making a deal with the devil."

She bent down to snap off Lola's leash. "There's no call for sassiness, young lady."

"Sorry. It's just he wanted me to know that they'll be here soon."

Her scrunch softened slightly. "How lovely. I'll make sure to have some refreshments prepared."

"No, it's really fine. You don't need to—"

She held up a ruby-nailed finger. "Sarah dear, there's

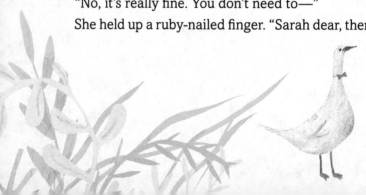

a right way and a wrong way to do everything in life. It is *always* right to make people feel welcome. And it is *always* right to feed them when they're hungry. People appreciate kindness. Remember that."

I knew way better than to argue. "Okay, fine. Thanks, Gran," I said, toeing off my sneakers and socks and letting the deliciously cool air of the house waft over my sweaty toes. Thank goodness there was at least one A/C in the Spot that was still working!

Lola trotted behind us as we made our way to the living room. Gran led the way, which meant I was able to check my phone one more time without her catching me. Still no answer from Mombo.

Grandad was napping in his leather armchair by the picture window, the exact same spot I left him two days ago. Only today he wasn't in his robe and slippers, which I hoped was a sign he was feeling better. One of those twenty-four-hour news channels was flickering across the TV screen and he was clutching the remote control to his chest like a teddy bear.

Gran marched over to the window and threw open the curtains.

"Goodness me," Grandad exclaimed, startling awake and blinking at the sudden flood of daylight. "What are you doing, Lillian?"

"Sorry to disturb you, darling, but Sarah has lost her duck. We must all do what we can to help her find it. Your job is to keep an eye on the shoreline. In case it's out there swimming. Can I leave that responsibility to you?"

Grandad swung around in his chair and caught my gaze. "You lost Webster?" he asked, his jaw dropping in alarm.

I nodded, biting my lip to keep my voice from cracking. "He . . . he was there one second and then he was just gone." I swallowed hard and hugged my stomach. Grandad turned back and gazed across the coastline at the craggy rocks. "Well. I'm sure he'll find his way back soon. Where would he want to be, if not with you?"

"Yes, that's what I believe too," Gran said, wrestling the remote out of his hand and clicking off the TV. "She treats that duck like a prince."

Grandad sat up straighter and smoothed the hem of his shirt over his round belly. "Of course, I'm happy to be on Webster patrol in the meantime. Oh, look!" he cried, pointing to the water. "Is that him?"

My heart gave a hopeful leap as I followed the direction of his finger to a small white object floating on the waves. I squinted and covered my eyes from the glare of the afternoon sun.

"No, Grandad. That's just a seagull."

"Oh. How about that one?"

"That one's a fishing buoy," I sighed.

Grandad fumbled for his glasses and slid them on. "Ah. So it is," he said, frowning at the water.

"Thank you for your vigilance, William. Keep up the good work. Sarah, wait here with your grandfather. I'll go get you something a bit drier and a lot cleaner to wear."

I went over to his chair and perched my behind on the armrest. Grandad's arm circled my back and I leaned against his shoulder. His big wrinkled hand covered mine and gave it a squeeze. "Hey, do you ever miss the old beach?" I asked him.

"Yes, of course. This house was built to make the most of that view. I used to watch the tides come and go from this very window. Sand, skies, water as far as the eye could see. It was spectacular, while we had it. However, I've learned there's no point grieving for what's gone."

Really? Grandad was one of the smartest people I knew, but that just didn't make sense. "If you love something, isn't it normal to miss it when it's gone?"

"Yes, of course. But if you spend too much time dwelling on what you've lost, you might not notice what remains in its place. Sometimes those things can be just as wonderful. In a different way."

I stared out at the grey, craggy rocks and jagged stones and wondered what anyone could possibly think was good about them. Grandad must have sensed what was going through my head.

"We wouldn't have any of those marvellous tide pools if the beach was still here. Think of all those afternoons we spent together combing over them, discovering treasures. We'd have missed them all if we'd been lazing around on a beach."

I never really thought of it that way. But I guess he had a point.

A moment later, Gran walked back in carrying a neatly folded pile of dry clothes — all of which, put together, created what was quite possibly the most Grandma-ish outfit in the universe. A pair of pastel-green slacks, yellow golf shirt and peach-coloured cashmere cardigan sweater. The only thing missing was a powder-blue sun visor and a pair of knitting needles. To top the style-bomb off, everything was two sizes too short for me. I suppose I could have just stayed in my own smelly, sweat-drenched clothes. But after the heartbreak of losing Webster, I honestly didn't have enough energy left in my emotion-drained body to care what I wore, let alone argue with Gran. So I just said thank you and went to the bathroom to change, after Grandad promised he'd keep his eyes peeled for Webster.

When I came out, Gran looked delighted. "There. That's much better," she said, chucking me under the chin. "Now you can be comfortable and focus on finding your duck." She opened her hands and waved me over for a hug. I stepped forward and let myself relax into the comfort of her soft arms.

"Hey, you know that painting you keep hidden under the bed?" I asked after a minute.

She paused. "Yes. Why?"

"I think you should bring it out." I pulled back and pointed to the empty space on the wall beside the picture window. "And hang it right there. So Grandad will have something nice to look at again."

Gran looked at me like I'd lost my mind. "That's impossible. Do you know how valuable that painting is?"

"Um, no."

"It's priceless. Why, every thief in the country would be after it if they knew it was here. It simply wouldn't be safe to hang it out in the open."

"So, sell it then. And use the money to travel around the world."

She clucked her tongue dismissively. "I could never."

"Paris. New York City. New Zealand. Or you could go on safari and see actual real-life elephants . . ."

"You're being ridiculous."

"But what's the point of having something precious if you can't enjoy it?"

She swatted my words away like a swarm of flies. "Stuff and nonsense. You kids say the strangest things sometimes."

I'd decided it was probably a good time to change the subject. "Any luck reaching my mother?" I asked. I'd stolen a peek at my phone while I was in the bathroom. Still no reply from Mombo on my end.

"She was in a meeting when I called the shop. But I'll keep trying. In the meantime, I have a bit of good news. While you were changing out of those sweaty clothes, I made a call to the chief of police."

I had to think for a second. "Old Mr. Amiel? With the scooter from two houses down?"

"Yes, that's right. He was terribly upset to hear about your duck. He's putting out an advisory about it right now."

"Really?" For the first time since I lost Webster, I could feel my spirits lifting a little bit.

She smiled. "Yes, really. He said it's unusual to issue an alert about a pet. But because it was registered as a

140

support animal, he'll make an exception. Isn't that wonderful?"

It was way more than wonderful. With the police
out looking for him, he couldn't possibly be missing for
much longer.

Could he?

D Stands for What?

The doorbell rang, sending Lola into a barking, leaping, snorting tizzy.

"Who could that be?" Gran said, her pencilled eyebrows shooting up.

"I think it must be the kids from my camp. Remember? They're coming here for the search party." I sprinted down the hall to answer it. Madz and JD were standing on the front stoop, bodies dripping with sweat and faces oozing concern. My heart flooded with gratitude. "Come on, you guys," I said, herding Lola back with my foot as I waved them in. "Quick. It's nice and cool in here!"

"Awesome," JD said, brushing past me. "Swaggy outfit." I knew by the telltale smirk tugging at his lips that he was dying to tease me about my grandma clothes. I could only guess he was holding back out of respect for Webster.

Madz bumped her shoulder up to mine. "You doing okay?"

I shrugged and glanced down at my toes. "Ish."

"Any word about Webster yet?"

"Nothing." It had been just over an hour since he'd gone missing. How did it already feel like days?

"All right, then let's get down to work." With a snap of her fingers, Madz took off down the main hall. "Got any recent photos of Webster you can text me? I'm going to make a whack of posters."

Her legs were nowhere near as long as mine, but I still found myself struggling to keep up.

Gran stood aside as we buzzed past her in the hall. Her nose wrinkled as she took in the scent of sweat-drenched clothes. She held up a warning finger, as if she was about to object. But Madz was moving too fast.

"Sorry, did you say posters?" I asked, hurrying along at her heels.

"For sure. Full size and full colour. With his cute little face on it. And your phone number so anyone who's seen him will know where to call. We'll cover the town in them!" Madz paused in front of the dining room. "Can we set up headquarters in here?"

I stopped walking and spun around, looking for Gran's approval.

She sighed and gave a nervous nod. "I suppose it would be fine. As long as you don't make a mess."

"Great," Madz said. She marched into the room,

plunked herself down at the head of the table — the place Grandad always sits in — and waved us over.

Gran hovered in the doorway, watching us warily. JD took the seat to the right of Madz, nodding his agreement with the plan. "Posters will definitely help. Generating good word of mouth is an excellent strategy for success."

"And we'll print up some awesome flyers too." Madz snapped her fingers. "Can you send me that photo asap?"

"Okay. Yeah." Taking the seat on the other side of her, I pulled out my phone and messaged her the most recent pic I had of Webster — the pink bow tie photo I'd taken of him this morning.

"This is all good," JD said, flipping open a notepad and scribbling down words. "Flyers are a very effective marketing tool," he added, pointing the tip of his pen at me. "Gets your info right into people's hands."

"And, ooooh!" Madz sucked in a breath and clapped her hands. "Maybe some T-shirts? Black with white Webster faces. I can get started on the graphic right now." She shrugged off her backpack, slid out a silver laptop and opened it up. Her fingers attacked the keyboard like a concert pianist.

"Think we should offer some kind of reward?" she

asked, never even looking up from the screen. "You know, to motivate local peeps to help look for him?"

I stared at her in amazement. I knew JD had business experience. But who knew Madz was such a planner? He must have been thinking the same thing as me because he pulled off his glasses and leaned in to peer at her closely with those dark brown eyes. Almost like he was seeing her for the very first time. I felt a twinge of something deep in my chest. Definitely not jealousy, okay? Don't even go there.

"Too bad you didn't make a run for student council this year," he said. "We really could have used an idea person like you."

Madz glanced up from the screen and made an air fart noise with her lips. "Meh. The kind of changes *I'd* want to make happen outside the box."

"Okay. But what about joining the young politicians club? It's non-partisan. You could create your own platform."

"Thanks, but no thanks," she said, turning her attention back to her laptop. "That sounds like exactly the kind of thing my parents would *want* me to do. Doesn't fit into my whole revenge scheme, ya know?" She stopped typing for a second and glanced up at the wall. "Whoa. Are those *baby spoons*?"

"Yeah. Well, teaspoons actually. My grandmother collects them." My voice dropped to a low whisper. "It's weird, I know."

"It's freaking awesome is what it is!" Madz said, taking a photo of the display case behind my head with her phone. "Why didn't you tell me your grandmother was a cool collector-lady?"

My eyes darted to the hallway, where I knew Gran was still listening in. She must have appreciated the compliment because her cheeks were flushed pink and she was beaming from ear to ear.

"I'll go get you kids some snacks," she said, backing away from the doorway and floating off toward the kitchen.

"Okay! Here we go!" Madz flipped the computer around so we could see what she'd done. "How's this for effective marketing?"

It was my photo of Webster on a Lost Pet poster with *Have You Seen this Duck?* typed across the top. He looked so small and adorable, and his round little eyes seemed to be staring right through the screen and into mine.

My heart jumped into my throat. "That's just, so great," I gasped. At this rate, between the posters, flyers and police alert, I was almost convinced we'd have him back before dinner. "I . . . just . . . thanks."

She smiled her tabby-cat smile. "It's nothing. I just need a few more details from you so I can finish it off. Then I'll move on to the T-shirt graphic."

"You guys are the best. I . . . I just need him back. So bad. I don't know what I'd do without him."

JD reached across the table and tugged on the sleeve of my cardigan. "We're happy to help, Mac. That's what friends are for."

It occurred to me that I didn't mind when he called me Mac so much anymore. Actually, I kind of liked it. It was sort of sweet. Like, a name only he was allowed to use. I took a deep breath and let it out slowly.

"Webster helped me get through a rough time in my life," I explained, my voice cracking a bit over that last part.

From the silence bubble that had taken over the room, they both knew I was talking about Papa. I swallowed hard, then flipped through my phone and clicked open FindYourPeeps. "I haven't seen him since I was two and a half," I added, passing it across the table to JD. "It felt like a good time to try something like this."

JD and Madz leaned into each other and huddled over my phone. I listened to my stomach stress-gurgling while I waited for them to finish. "Wow. So, did they find him for you?" he asked, looking up from the screen.

I swallowed hard. "Well, uh, I haven't actually started the search yet. They're asking for lots of information I don't have."

"Like what? Maybe we can help," Madz said, flipping her computer back around again. "I mean, while we're making all these posters for Webster anyway. What's a few more? What do you need?" Her fingers started flying over the keyboard again.

I waved my hands to stop her. "I really don't think posters are going to help with this one. My father's been gone for almost ten years now. I mean . . . I don't even know what he looks like."

"Did you try Google?" JD asked.

I dropped my forehead into my hands. "Try looking up Lasagna and see how many bazillion hits you get."

"What about Facebook?"

"Of course. I'm not stupid." I leaned over and pointed at the long list of questions on the screen. "Any of these things would help. I just don't know where to find the answers. And I can't exactly ask my mother . . ." I really didn't want to get into all the reasons why *that* would be a bad idea. Luckily, neither of them pressed me to say more.

"Well, I can ask *my* mom," JD said, his eyes brightening. "She says she knew him, right? Maybe she can remember something helpful. Don't worry, I won't tell her what it's for." He bent over his notepad and started writing furiously. "Tell me again the details you need to know?"

I shook my head and clicked off my phone. "Thanks, but it's okay. I got this."

"Really. I don't mind."

"Really, it's okay," I insisted, flumping back in my seat.

JD stopped writing and looked up. I saw him exchange worried glances with Madz.

"Why won't you let us help you?"

"My dude! This is what friends are for."

I squeezed my eyes shut so tightly it hurt. "I'm really not so sure you guys should be my friends," I mumbled, shifting uncomfortably in my seat. My two-sizes-too-small Grandma clothes were suddenly riding up in all the wrong places. "I think about leaving. A lot."

"What? Like, camp?"

"No." The next word came out before I even knew I was going to say it. "Town. If this app doesn't work, I'm going to go find him myself," I added. "With Webster, of course. He'll be back by then."

Madz's eyes grew so big, I thought they might pop

out of her face. "You mean *run away*?"

I wanted to say more. But my throat was too tight to get another word out. All I could do was nod.

Her hand flew across the table and clutched my arm. "Can I come with you?" she hissed.

"Knock-knock! Who'd like some refreshments?"

The door flew open and Gran entered the dining room carrying a heavy snack-filled tray with Lola yipping and scampering at her heels. I was so startled to see her, I almost fell off my chair.

"Holy crust!" I gasped. "You scared me."

"No need for vulgarities, Sarah," Gran said, teetering dangerously as she tried to sidestep Lola.

JD shot to his feet and took the tray from her. It was loaded with cookies, chips, salsa, three glasses and a pitcher of iced lemonade. "Thank you, Mrs. Cameron. This looks great."

She dusted off her hands and surveyed the room. "Right, then. There are plenty of coasters and napkins for you to use. Does anybody need anything else?"

"No. We're good, Gran."

"Fine. I'll go check in on your grandfather now. Excuse me."

"Hey, love your spoons!" Madz called out as she walked away.

As soon as she was out of earshot, JD turned back to me. His dark eyes suddenly looked more like burning molten lava. *Oh yikes. Was he angry?*

"Listen up! It's too late to back out now, Mac," he barked, drawing an invisible air triangle in the space between us. "See this? Newsflash: we're *already* friends. Nothing you can say will change that."

"Really?" I crossed my arms in front of my cashmere-cardiganed chest. "How can you call yourself my friend when I don't even know your middle name?"

He squeezed his eyes shut tight. "Fine. If that's what you need, I'll tell you guys what the *D* stands for."

An excited little shriek flew out of my mouth. "For real?" I wasn't expecting him to give in that easily.

"Yeah. But you have to cross your heart and promise not to laugh. Okay?"

Madz and I drew matching *X*s over our chests.

"And now swear on your mothers' everlasting souls."

"What?" I shook my head. "I'm not doing that. Sorry."

Madz brought her hand down onto the table with a slam so hard, the teaspoons rattled in their cases. "I'll swear for both of us. Okay?"

"Okay. And you can't tell anyone. Promise? Especially not at school."

She grabbed a fistful of his sleeve and gave it a yank. "You're killing me here!"

"Fine. It's . . ." he gritted his teeth like he was in pain. "I can't believe I'm doing this."

Madz yanked a bit harder. "Give it up, bro!"

"It's . . . gah!" Shaking off her grip, he grabbed his notepad and pen.

The air was thick with suspense as he scribbled something down. When he was finished, he shoved it across the table, dropped his face onto his folded arms, and waited for us to read it.

Madz and I lunged for it at the same time. But my super-long arms won easily.

#victoryismine

I unfolded the paper and held it up to my face.

"What does it say? Let me see!" Madz demanded. I cupped a hand over my mouth and passed it to her obediently. I'd promised I wouldn't laugh. And I felt guilty even thinking about laughing when Webster was out there missing. But it was taking super-human muscle power to keep the giggles in.

"Hold up," I said, working to keep my voice steady. "Your parents named you *Joshua Danger Granger?*"

"It's an ancestral name on my mom's side. Like, a really old tradition. Every boy in her family has had it.

Since the Dark Ages or something."

Madz had to cover her mouth with the neck of her T-shirt. But I could still see the smile in her eyes. "Were they thinking you'd grow up to be a comic book villain?"

"I told you, *Danger*'s a tradition. It didn't matter if it went well with my last name or not. They couldn't break the streak." He swivelled in his chair so he was facing me. "So, what's *your* middle name, Mac?"

I took a chip off the tray and nibbled on the edges. "Mine isn't nearly as exciting as yours."

"Still. You promised."

I was about to tell him but suddenly there was a flurry of footsteps and Mombo burst into the room, her blue eyes wild with worry. She didn't say a word. She just rushed to my side and wrapped me up in a hug so tight, I couldn't tell where she ended and I began.

"Webster . . . He's—"

"I know. We'll find him."

"What if—"

"No what-ifs. We'll find him."

I don't know what happened in that particular moment, but I felt something fragile suddenly go *snap* inside me. And for the first time in hours, I let myself break down and cry.

HELP! HELP! Lost Pet!

Have You Seen this Duck?

Male, White Pekin Duck, 9 years old

About 10 pounds

Name: Webster Lasagna

Last seen: leaving the BBTS Community Centre on Wednesday morning

Easily scared but will respond to gentle voices and birdseed

If you have seen him or know where he is please, please, please phone Sarah's cell

472 555 0387

Cash money reward for this duck's safe return!

Dear Papa,

I lost Webster today.

My new friends from cooking camp are helping me search for him.

You never knew Webster. But I think you'd like my friends . . . if you ever met them.

Sometimes I really hate you for leaving. And then I feel guilty. Like, what kind of horrible kid could possibly hate their own parent?

But are you technically still my parent if you're never here when I need you?

Your confused daughter,
Sarah

Speechless

I spent the night relearning a painful truth: *Nothing's harder than waiting for news about someone you love.*

Mombo and I stayed up until midnight going over all the places Webster might be and brainstorming different ways to find him and bring him home. Some of our best ideas included:

— dropping a birdseed trail leading from the harbour to our apartment building

— a front-page article in the *BBTS Weekly Post*

— setting up an anonymous 24-hour tip hotline

— calling in sniffer dogs

— hiring a professional duck caller

— consulting a psychic specializing in missing persons and/or pets

Of course, I didn't sleep a wink after she came to tuck me into bed. And it had nothing to do with our still-busted air conditioning and everything to do with my missing roommate. I tossed and turned and sobbed his name into my pillow for so many hours, until the point it felt like my heart might actually implode from sadness. The next morning, when Mombo came into my room to check on me, I was a teary, sweaty, exhausted, rumpled mess.

"Oh goodness, Sarah," she said, sprinting to my side and reaching out to feel my forehead. I wanted to tell her I was heartbroken, not sick. I wanted to ask if she'd heard anything about Webster. I wanted to see if we could go down to the harbour to look for him again, in case he'd returned overnight. But when I opened my mouth, nothing came out but a weak puff of air. I couldn't speak. All the words I wanted to say were clogged in my throat. And as hard as I tried, I couldn't make them budge.

Mombo must have read my thoughts about Webster. "Chief Amiel at the police station left us a message this morning," she said. "There have been a few leads . . . a couple of sightings in nearby communities. He's confident today will bring good news." She smoothed her hand over my nest of curls, her blue eyes wide with concern. "You must've cried yourself hoarse. Let me make you some tea, darling. I'm sure it'll help soothe your throat."

She brewed the tea and I drank two steaming mugfuls mixed with honey and lemon. But it didn't make a smidge of a difference. My voice was still missing. And there was a hot, squeezy pain deep inside my belly that wouldn't go away. Mombo chewed nervously on her bottom lip as she watched me blinking back tears and struggling to push out some words. I could guess what she was thinking — the last time this happened was ten years ago.

She glanced over her shoulder at the glowing digits on the microwave clock. "Maybe you should stay home from camp today. You might feel better if you could catch up on your sleep. What do you think? I could come check on you during my lunch break?"

I shook my head. As much as I hated the idea of going anywhere without Webster beside me, the thought of being all alone here in this overheated apartment, without him or Mombo, was too sad to even consider. I needed distractions. I needed my friends.

I needed to go to camp.

I got dressed in record time, not even pausing to think about what I was wearing, or the sleep knots in my hair, or the dark worry circles under my eyes. Those little things had no meaning with Webster gone. I barely even noticed the burning sun when we stepped outside our building. Or the stale heat of the car. All I could think about was Webster's sad, empty little bed beside mine. And the fear spreading inside me like a virus.

What if he's trapped? Or lost? Or hurt? Or . . . or . . .
I wouldn't let myself finish that thought. Every time I came even a little bit close, I had to pinch my earlobes hard to chase it away.

On our way to camp, we swung by the harbour to look for him, but no luck. Although we passed at least two dozen Webster posters on the drive to the community centre. Madz and JD must have spent hours putting them up around the Spot last night. My heart swelled at the sight of Webster's sweet face and his cute little bow tie. How was it possible that photo was taken just one day ago?

Mombo looked worried as she kissed me goodbye for the day.

"I'll text you immediately if I hear any news, okay?" She squeezed my hand a little harder than normal. "And you'll text me if you hear anything also?"

I nodded, pushed open the door, and stepped out of the car. The mayonnaise walls of room 113 seemed more yellow than usual this morning. Sick and gluey, like the gloppy stuff you find in potato salad left out in the heat. I could practically smell it as I took my place beside Madz at the counter. I caught her gaze as I peeled off my backpack and let it drop to my feet with a plop. She watched me warily.

"You're not about to hurl, are you?"

I forced out a weak smile to let her know she didn't have to worry. Her black shirt of the day read *Tween Idle*, which I might have thought was funny on a different kind of day. I'd been hoping to see the Webster graphic she was working on last night, but I guess she didn't have time to get it printed yet.

"JD and I got all the posters done and set up. The lady at the print shop was so upset to hear about Webster, she donated the paper! Isn't that great? There's two hundred of them all over town. And I put out a social media blast and handed out a bunch of flyers this morning. Someone's gonna spot him soon. Keep your ringer volume on in case they call, 'kay?"

I nodded to let her know I agreed with all of the above.

She tilted her head and peered at me closely. "You got laryngitis?"

Before I could even attempt a reply, the door flew open and in strode JD.

"Hey!" he said, bounding over to where we were standing. "I got some deets from my mom over breakfast this morning. She remembered a few things about your father that might help." He reached into his back pocket and handed me an envelope. "I wrote it all down so I wouldn't forget. But you, ah, might want to read it later. When you're alone. You know?"

I took the envelope from him and held it carefully in both hands. Like it was made of glass instead of paper.

Holy crust. This could be it. The key to finding Papa after all these years.

Madz's hand landed gently on my shoulder. "Dude. You're shaking."

Was I?

Deciding to take JD's advice and read it later, I tucked the envelope into the front pocket of my back-pack. That's the moment Gigi made her usual fashionably late entrance. Except there was nothing usual about the way she looked today. She was dressed in sweats instead of a sundress and her hair was pulled back in a messy ponytail. For the first time all week, she wasn't wearing her false eyelashes or her bright red lipstick, and I was startled at how young she looked. Like, she could easily pass for a kid our age if she wanted to. Trudging to her desk, she slid dejectedly into the chair and released a low moan of despair. Anyone would think *she* was the one who'd just lost her best friend.

"Today we cook the onion soup *française*," she mumbled in a voice so weak I had to strain to hear it. "I beg of you kids," she added, holding up a finger, "please for *once* try to make this *one* dish a success. I have been told my job depends on it."

"What does that mean?" JD asked, narrowing his eyes. "They're not threatening to fire you . . . are they?"

She dropped her forehead onto her desk with a soft thud. "They say I am failing as a teacher," she groaned into the wood. "They say you have learned nothing all week. I say this is not my fault. Too bad, they do not agree."

Madz glanced at me and JD. "Sooooo, what exactly does that mean for us?" she asked, twirling a finger around one of her red-streaked pigtails.

"We'll still get our certificate though, right?" JD cut in. "That's what the camp brochure promised when we signed up."

Gigi rocked her head from side to side. "The feast is scheduled for tomorrow," she mumbled. "If they do not fire me first. But I fear it will turn out to be *un grand désastre*. Unless you three can somehow learn to cook by then, we must do something."

Mombo had already booked off the hour for tomorrow's big finale lunch. Was it about to get cancelled?

JD did not look happy with this news. At all. He untied his apron and threw it onto the counter. He was so upset, his glasses were starting to fog up. "You're the teacher," he said. "Maybe you should try harder to teach us."

"Yeah!" Madz chimed in. "And maybe if you hadn't been so mean to Webster all week, we'd be more willing to help you out of this mess."

Gigi lifted her head and stared at us in amazement. "You kids . . . You would help *me*?" Before she could say any more, there was a knock at the classroom door. It squeaked open halfway and Cousin Jerry poked his head in.

"Sorry to interrupt the lesson, but this is rather urgent. There's someone here with a new piece of, uh . . . duck evidence."

Gigi sat up straighter and smoothed down the messy wisps of her ponytail. "Okay, yes. Of course, Monsieur Cameron," she said, waving her hand. "Let them in."

Jerry stepped aside and pulled open the door all the way. A police officer strode into the room, her black boots clomping heavily across the linoleum floor. Finally she stopped in front of Gigi's desk and faced us. She was wearing white rubber medical gloves. There was a paper bag in her hands and a frown hard enough to cut diamonds across her face. Her gaze immediately zoomed in on me. "Are you Sarah Lasagna?"

All I could manage was a feeble nod. It felt like my

stomach was free-falling out of my body. I knew whatever this lady was about to say wasn't going to be good.

"Sorry to report that we haven't located your animal yet. However, we have found something." She reached into the bag, pulled out a small white object, and held it up for us to see. "This was spotted by a jogger earlier this morning near the site of the old beach. Are you able to identify it for us?"

I recognized it immediately, of course.

Duck-sized, custom-ordered in bulk from the internet.

But no Webster attached.

You and Me Day

As you can probably guess, I was way too upset after that to make soup.

It was so hard not to break down and cry in front of everyone. Struggling to hold back tears, I texted Mombo about Webster's diaper. She had to turn around and come right back and pick me up at camp. I didn't ask her how she managed to get out of work. Closing the shop is a really big deal because it means nobody gets paid that day. Pretty sure that won't do much to improve Jill's opinion of Webster.

JD and Madz were upset to see me leave. They vowed they wouldn't stop handing out flyers until Webster was found. Even Gigi seemed sad to see me go. "Eh, Mademoiselle Lasagna," she said softly as I passed her desk on my way out the door. "I am very sorry about your duck."

Something in her eyes told me she meant it. I'm not sure if she was saying sorry for calling him a beast. Or sorry that he was lost. Or maybe both. Either way, I appreciated it.

On the drive home, I kept busy trying to cure my-self of a stubborn case of stress hiccups. I could tell Mombo was stressing too because she was chattering nonstop about the weather to fill the awkward silence. Something-something-something about the heat wave and how the blah-blah-blah was predicting a big storm might happen any minute and bring the yada-yada sys-tem we were all praying for. But I was barely listening and it must have been like talking to a wall, which prob-ably upset her even more, because two streets from our apartment, she surprised me by pulling over to the curb.

I shot her a look that said *what are you doing?*

She answered with a mischievous wink. "What do you say we make it a 'You and Me Day,' darling?"

Without waiting for an answer, she flipped the radio to my favourite station and turned the car around. Ten minutes later, we pulled up in front of the orthodontist's office.

I gave her a look that said *really*?

"Come on. Let's start by getting you those horribly vulgar elastics you've been asking for," she said with a laugh.

After that, we stopped for ice cream and she treated me to a double scoop of my favourite, mint chocolate chip, with sprinkles and cookie crumbs and gummies (even though those were the number one food on my orthodontist's "banned for braces" list, but Mombo said it was okay just this once 'cause this was a special occasion). Then we took a long walk along the shoreline while melting ice cream dribbled onto our fingers, and we had to slurp it off in a way that would have sent my well-mannered grandmother into a fainting spell. We were both sweat-covered, sticky, drippy hot messes.

I don't remember ever seeing Mombo looking so utterly dishevelled and un-daintified, and I actually caught myself smiling once or twice. And then I felt guilty for smiling. How could I be experiencing happiness when Webster was out there all alone and possibly lost to me forever?

I could feel my stress hiccups prepping for a comeback. But I couldn't warn Mombo because my voice was still stuck. I was trying not to worry too much, but what if my voice decided not to come back, like, ever again?

I needed Webster to comfort me. And to work his speech therapy magic.

We walked in silence, nibbling slowly on the ends of our cones while I kept my eyes peeled for Webster. My phone was clutched so tightly in my free hand, it was getting sweaty and I had to wrap it in a napkin so it wouldn't short-circuit. I guess I could have just put it in my pocket. But I was too scared I might miss an important call about Webster if I did. Although to be honest, I had no idea if I was going to manage to get any words out when that happened.

I was checking it every few minutes. There was a whole string of texts from Madz that I should probably reply to at some point.

Hey
Any news?
Omg
Ur not gonna believe what ur missing at camp today
It's epic
Call me asap
Where r u??

And one from JD. *imu*

Did that mean what I think it meant?

If so, was he waiting for me to reply? I typed the same three letters back to him and almost hit *send*, but chickened out and erased them before actually going through with it. It felt like betraying Webster to write *imu* to someone else while he was still missing. The envelope JD had given me was tucked safely into the front pocket of my backpack. I was dying to open it and see what details he'd found out about Papa. But I couldn't do that in front of Mombo.

"Good grief, I think today might be the hottest one yet," she said, daintily dabbing her sweaty forehead with her napkin before balling it up and dropping it into the nearest bin. "I've noticed you're still not talking, darling."

I shrugged and tossed mine in right after hers. *Nice detective work, Captain Obvious.*

"I'm worried," she added after a minute.

I took her hand and gave it a squeeze, which was our secret silent code for *I love you*, left over from the days I was a little kid who couldn't remember how to speak. She raised my fingernails up to her face. "Tsk. Your cuticles are a mess. What do you say . . . should we go get manicures next?"

I shook my head. Still holding her hand, I turned around and led her back to the parking lot. I was hot and tired and sad and I wanted to go home. "You and Me Day" just wasn't the same without Webster. I was relieved she didn't try to change my mind.

As soon as we got back to our apartment, I kicked off my sandals and handed Mombo my phone so she could answer it if an important call came in. Then I crashed into my bed for a nap. I have no idea how long

I slept, but when I finally woke up, I felt a lot better. And full of energy. I didn't want to sit around feeling sorry for myself anymore. I was ready to search the world until I tracked down Webster and brought him home where he belonged. Bolting out of bed, I went to find Mombo.

I froze in my tracks when I saw her. She was sitting at the kitchen table with my cell phone in front of her and a pained look in her eyes. It felt like I was watching in slow motion as she held it up for me to see the screen. My stomach turned a wobbly somersault.

FindMyPeeps was open. Along with the message: *Welcome back, Sarah. Ready to complete your search?*

All the Words

"Something you'd like to tell me, darling?"

Mombo's delicate features were drooping with disappointment. She looked like a person who'd just been stabbed in the back by their best friend. My gaze slunk down to the chipped nail polish on my big toes.

She sighed wearily. "Maybe you want to start by explaining what you're doing with this app?"

I opened my mouth to answer, but couldn't manage to force out more than a squeak.

"Maybe my mother was right," she said, her voice cracking slightly. "Maybe you are too young for the responsibility that comes with this technology."

Well, that got all my defences up. I shook my head defiantly and reached across the table to retrieve my phone. But Mombo scooped it up and held it to her chest. The muscles in her jaw were clenched.

"I just can't believe you'd go and do this behind my back," she said. Her brows were doing that twitchy thing and I could see her blinking back tears. "Really, Sarah . . . how could you betray me like this?"

Suddenly, it was like that hot, squeezy pain that had been pinching its way through my belly all day caught fire and flared up into my throat. And a second later all my emotions exploded out of me, like bottled-up fizz from a soda that someone shook too hard.

"Y-you know w-what?" I croaked. "I didn't want to go b-behind your back! But you didn't give me a ch-ch-choice. Why did you have to k-keep Papa such a secret from me all these years?"

Mombo dropped my phone onto the table with a thunk. "I . . . I was trying to protect you," she said, staring at me with moon-sized eyes.

"From what?"

She reached out to take my hand. "Darling, there's so much you don't—"

I jumped back holding my hands firmly to my sides. "Stop. Don't darling me! What kind of mother makes their only child feel like a criminal for wanting to know more about her own father?"

She leaned over and clutched her forehead, like she was trying to save it from falling off her face. "Is that how I've made you feel?" she asked, her voice tiny as a flea.

"Was it your fault?" I demanded. "Did he leave because of you?"

"No. No, of course not. How could you—"

"Well, if it wasn't you, then it had to be me."

Mombo's face softened. "Sarah. My love, it didn't have anything to do with you." She paused and glanced at the ceiling. The tiny muscles around her mouth quivered as she searched for the right words. "Believe me, your father loved you as best as he knew how."

"If he loved me, then why did he leave? And why doesn't he ever come back to see me?"

Pushing back her chair, Mombo stood up slowly and walked off toward her bedroom. I was sure that was her way of signalling the conversation was over. But a few seconds later, she surprised me by returning with a shoebox in her hands. She placed it on the table in front of me and lifted the lid. I stepped forward to get a look. Inside was a stack of envelopes. My jaw dropped.

"I know you've been writing to him," she said softly.

"How . . . how did you . . ."

"A blank envelope into the same mailbox every single day for over two years? The postmaster finally had enough, and decided to open one. It's a small town, darling. He figured out who 'your daughter, Sarah' was pretty easily."

She pushed the stack of letters toward me. I glanced at Webster's empty chair, wishing he was here to help make this better. I closed my eyes for a second and imagined him nuzzling his cheek against mine.

"Why, Sarah? You must have realized he wouldn't receive them."

"I don't know," I finally managed to whisper. "I guess it felt like . . . the closest thing to an actual conversation."

"Oh."

"How long have you known?"

"About six months."

"And did you read them?"

"A few, yes."

Ouch. That was hard to hear. I glanced up to meet her gaze. "And you didn't think to say anything to me? This whole time?"

"I'm sorry. I guess I thought you'd be angry with me if you knew."

"Well, congrats. I am angry!" I stomped my foot for emphasis, knowing — but not really caring — that it was the kind of thing only a bratty little kid would do. "And you know what else I am? Tired of all your secrets!" I held out my palm. "Can I have my phone back, please?"

My bottom lip was trembling out of control and I knew I was on the verge of a meltdown. All I wanted was the chance to implode in privacy. A few seconds passed before she let out a sad sigh and placed my phone gently into my outstretched hand. I turned around on my heel and stomped off to my room, slamming the door behind me so hard, my African Elephant poster slid off the wall and landed face-down onto my bed.

I dropped to the floor, tore open the zipper of my backpack and pulled out the envelope JD had given me at camp. I'd waited all day to read this, I wasn't going to wait another second. If I couldn't find Webster, I would find my father. One or the other. I couldn't live without both.

I ripped it open, ready to gobble up JD's notes. My eyes landed on the first line. His name.

Niccolò.

Papa's name is Niccolò.

"Mr. Niccolò Lasagna," I said to myself, covering my mouth to keep my voice from carrying through the thin walls.

I wanted to hear myself say all of our names together. To hear them out loud, side by side in the same sentence.

"The Lasagna family: Caroline, Sarah and Niccolò. Niccolò and Sarah Lasagna."

I rolled the words around in my mouth, like a candy

I wanted to make last as long as possible.

"This is my dad, Niccolò. Sure, you can call him, Nick. Or Nicky. Have you met my dad, Nick Lasagna?"

I scanned my eyes down the rest of the page, swirling all the new information about Papa around in my brain, attaching the details to the blurry memories I had left.

After a minute, I clicked on my phone and typed the new details into the blank spaces on the app.

Full name: Niccolò Lasagna
Height: 6 foot, 3 inches
Place of birth: Naples, Italy
Distinctive Features: peace sign tattoo on left bicep; burn scar on back of right hand
Hobbies and interests: sailing, fishing, photography, travel, yoga
Last known places of employment: Sonata Chartered Cruises, Blackhead by the Sea Weekly Post

It didn't look like much at all — just a scattering of words on a long list of unanswered questions. But maybe, hopefully, it would be enough to find him. I took a deep breath. *"Pronto,"* I whispered to absolutely nobody.

And then I clicked *Search.*

The screen froze. I could feel my heartbeat racing all the way up through my chest and into my ears, so loud I thought my eardrums might actually burst while I waited to see what would happen next. Seconds ticked by like hours until finally there was a flash and there it was — four names with four tiny, thumbnail photos attached.

Four men named Niccolò Lasagna. Right there. Rounded up for me in a neat little square package.

Chances are, one of them was probably my father.

I squinted at the thumbnail photos. The man in the second one was wearing glasses. And had dark hair.

Curly. Like mine.

Holy crumble.

The wish I'd made on every first star . . . The dream I played on repeat night after night . . . The one thing I'd obsessed about for years was suddenly right there. In my hands. I let out a terrified squeak, shut off my phone, and tossed it into the dark, dusty sliver of space deep under my bed. Then I pulled the covers up over my head and hiccupped myself to sleep.

Eye of the Storm

Pop, pop, pop — flashes of white light flooded my dreams. Moments later, I awoke with a scream as the sky came crashing down over my head. I bolted upright in bed just as a second round of thunder boomed around me. This one was so loud, I could feel it echoing in my bones. Kicking back my sheets, I ran to my window and peered outside. Rain was teeming down so hard the streets below looked like a river. Above our sleeping neighbourhood, grey clouds were crackling with electricity.

I watched the rain pour down until another ear-splitting crash and flash sent me diving back into my bed. The eye of the storm had to be right over our building.

"Webster!" I whimpered, pulling the sheet up over my head. "I need you, I need you, where are you, come back, pleasepleasepleasepleaseplease—"

I heard my door open and a flutter of shuffling footsteps and suddenly Mombo was there, lifting the sheet and crawling into bed beside me. She must have heard my scream.

"It's just a thunderstorm, darling," she said, gently wiping away my tears with the sleeve of her nightshirt.

I threw my arm around her neck and hugged her tight, our big argument from earlier tonight forgotten. "But he's never been outside in a storm before! What if the lightning hits him? How will he know how to keep safe?"

She stroked my sleep-tangled curls and spoke so calmly, I had to lower the volume of my crying to hear her. "He'll be okay," she crooned. "He's smart. And animals instinctively know what to do in a storm like this. Besides, ducks love the rain. Remember all those times we took him outside in the middle of a shower to play?"

I did, and found myself smiling through my tears at the memory: Mombo and me standing in the parking lot wearing our rain boots and slickers while Webster splashed from puddle to puddle, flapping his wings and quacking with joy.

I flinched as a new round of thunder rattled the walls. "But what if all this noise is scaring him? Maybe we should go check the harbour again?"

"Not in this storm, darling. It's too dark and it's not safe to be walking around when there's lightning. I promise, we'll head out first thing in the morning."

My room lit up with a bright white flash followed by

another deafening clap of thunder. I cupped my hands over my ears and buried my face in her hair. "Why would he leave me?"

I could feel the muscles in Mombo's arms tighten around me. I'm sure she was wondering if I was talking about Papa or Webster. To be honest, I wasn't really sure either.

"I can't live without him," I moaned. "I can't."

"Of course you can. If you had to. You're stronger than you know."

"No, no, no, I'm not!"

"Pets leave us eventually, darling. I know it's heartbreaking, but that's the way it has to be."

She was right, of course. Ducks don't live as long as humans. Webster was never going to be with me forever. But knowing that was true didn't make it any less painful to bear. I pulled back just enough so I could see her face. "Can I *hic* ask you something?" I whispered.

She nodded. "Of course."

"Promise not to get mad?"

"I'll do my best."

"No. You have to *hic* promise."

Her eyes narrowed warily. "Okay, fine. I promise."

I took a long, shaky breath. "If you knew I was writing to Papa, why didn't you *hic* put his address on those envelopes when you got them? So they could get delivered? So he could *hic* know I'm still thinking about him."

There was a long pause that sent my mind spinning off to all kinds of scary places. Through the darkness, I saw Mombo shake her head. "I couldn't do that, even if I'd wanted to, darling."

"Why not? Is he — did he . . . *hic* . . . ?" I couldn't bring myself to finish the question.

"No, no . . . hush, now." She took my hands in hers and squeezed. "It's just that I honestly don't know his address."

That was what I was hoping she'd say. But to me, it still wasn't a good enough reason.

"Couldn't you have at least tried to track down his *hic* address? Hire a detective or something? I mean, you must have a *hic* general idea of where he is in the world." I sniffled and swiped the back of my hand over my leaking eyes. "If it was me, and I had a daughter who was looking for her father, I would have *hic* tried harder."

She smoothed my damp hair away from my face. "You're right," she said. Her voice sounded rough, like she was fighting a cold. "Maybe I could have tried harder."

"What stopped you?"

I was trying to keep my volume down. Trying to keep my words from coming out too angry. But it was hard. My heart was overflowing with ten years of hurt. I needed an answer to that question. And tonight, for once in my life, I wasn't going to let Mombo off the hook.

After an agonizingly long minute, she spoke again. Her words crept across the dark space between us, tiny and thin as a parade of ants. "I suppose a part of me was afraid that he wouldn't care enough to write you back."

I swallowed a painful sob. That was hard to hear.

"And the other part of me . . ."

Mombo's voice suddenly shrunk to a whisper. I held my breath and waited. Her eyes were shining brightly through the darkness. Was she crying too?

". . . the other part of me was afraid that he would."

It Happened on a Fuzzy Morning

I don't remember what time it was when I finally fell back asleep. But the next thing I knew, fuzzy morning light was streaming through my window. I rolled onto my side, as memories from the night before came flickering back. And for a split second, I wondered if maybe that awful storm had been just a bad dream. My heart swelled with hope.

What if all of it was just a nightmare? What if this whole week never actually happened at all?

Rubbing the sleep from my eyes, I shot up and looked around the room for Webster. But when my gaze landed on his empty little bed, I knew it was all too real. I sunk back down onto my pillow with a flump. My gaze skipped over to the giant map of the world tacked up on the wall across from my bed. "Where are you?" I whispered softly.

Somewhere in the apartment, a phone was ringing. I glanced at my clock. It was a few minutes after six. Nobody ever called this early.

Did that mean . . . maybe . . .

Leaping out of bed, I threw open my door and raced down the hallway, just in time to hear Mombo's voice.

"You're kidding! Really?"

I found her standing in the kitchen wearing her bathrobe and slippers. I dashed to her side, clutching onto her arm so tight, my knuckles were turning white.

"My goodness! When?" Mombo exclaimed, clasping her forehead.

"What is it?" I begged, hopping up and down with suspense. "What's happening?"

She shook her head at me and held a finger to her lips. "Okay . . . yes. We're coming right now. Bye."

"Tell me!" I demanded, convinced I was going to leap out of my skin if she didn't answer. "Did someone find Webster?"

"No, darling," she said, staring down at the phone in her hand like it was one of those weird, confusing cubist paintings. "It's — you're not going to believe it."

"Who, then? Papa?"

"No." She looked up and caught my gaze. Her eyes were as wide and round as a pair of golf balls. "The beach. It's back."

Back to the Beach

I gasped when Mombo and I opened the front door of our building. It was like someone had dropped our town into a blender overnight. Roof tiles, garbage, twigs and snapped branches littered the ground, patio furniture sat overturned in the middle of the street, there was a recycling bin on the hood of a car and someone's soggy laundry line was hanging from the top of the big red maple tree beside the parking lot.

"Holy scrap!" I said, surveying the chaos. "That was one heck of a storm."

"I just hope nobody in town was hurt," Mombo said, covering her eyes from the glare of the morning sun. "At least it washed away that terrible heat wave." She was right. For the first time in what felt like forever, the air was fresh and cool again.

We took off in the direction of the water, side-stepping windblown trash and downed branches the entire way. I guess I didn't really know what to expect, so when we finally turned the corner to the harbour and saw what had happened, I almost fell over from the shock. Instead of the same ugly grey expanse of craggy rocks and stones that had lined the waterfront all these years, there was a long, beautiful, golden beach. So perfect and smooth, it was hard to believe it was real. I wish Webster was here to see this with me. He'd love it!

"Goodness gracious," Mombo said breathlessly. "It really is back."

I blinked a few times, trying to make sense of what was in front of me. My eyes were definitely seeing a beach, but my brain wasn't actually convinced it was there.

What was happening? Was this the same legendary beach that vanished all those years ago? Or a random new one that decided to drop in for a visit?

Did it even matter?

I had to touch it, to be sure it wasn't some kind of mirage or trick of the light. I ran over, kicked off my sandals and dug my feet into the soft, cool sand. It was still a little damp from last night's rain and it squished up deliciously between my toes. It was real! A spark of happiness lit up my insides and I had a sudden urge to lie down and bury myself head to toe in our brand-new, long-lost beach.

I looked around for Mombo. It wasn't even seven in the morning, but word about the beach must have spread pretty quick because there was a growing crowd of people gathering around the waterfront, each and every one of their faces looking just as gobsmacked as ours. There was an eerie hush in the air as people reached out with their hands and feet to touch the sand. It was almost like nobody wanted to make too much noise, just in case this was all a lovely dream we were collectively enjoying. Some stood back, staring in confusion, like they weren't sure what to do with a brand-new beach. Some went straight to the waterline, decorating the untouched sand with a flurry of footprints. A few people had flopped themselves out on the ground, arms and legs akimbo, staring up at the sky like human sand angels.

After a minute, I finally found Mombo. She was one of the angels.

I was about to go over and flop down beside her when JD appeared out of nowhere. "There you are!" he cried, clasping my shoulder. He was huffing and puffing like he'd just run a marathon and it took him a few seconds to catch his breath. His floppy carrot hair was a windblown mess. Behind his glasses, his eyes were wild with excitement. "I've been calling and texting you for the past hour. Didn't you check your phone?"

"Oops, sorry," I said, patting my shorts pockets to find it. That's when I suddenly remembered where it was: deep under my bed where I'd tossed it last night. Crumb. How could I have been so careless? What if I'd missed a call about Webster?

Before I could explain, JD turned and took off toward the water, dragging me along behind him. "Let's go," he cried.

Was he taking me for a swim? "Wait! Let me just grab my shoes."

"No time," he panted. "I gotta show you . . . I got here early to see the beach. I couldn't believe it when—"

"I know, right?" I said, wobbling a bit as I tried to keep pace with him. My bare feet weren't used to walking through sand. "I couldn't believe it either! I thought it was an optical illusion or something."

He glanced over his shoulder at me. "What? No . . . I'm not talking about the beach. Come on!"

Now he was full-out running. I struggled to keep up with him over the soft sand. "Slow down, JD!" I begged. "What's the big rush?"

Instead of an answer, he led me past the old lighthouse and around the bend to a small sandy cove, sheltered from the waves and away from the crowd.

My breath caught in my chest. Because there, paddling peacefully in the shallow water, was a trio of ducks.

One of them was wearing a pink bow tie.

Feather Butt

I sunk to my knees in the sand and held out my arms.

"Webster!"

His little head whipped around at the sound of my voice and I knew he must have spotted me, because a second later he was rising up out of the water, flapping his wings against the surface and letting out an excited honk. And then suddenly he was waddling up the shore toward me.

I reached out and pulled him into my arms and he snuggled his chin on my shoulder, his favourite spot. I could hear him clucking with happiness, and for a second it felt like no time had passed between us at all.

"Webster! Websie-Woo!" I gasped, holding him tight to my chest, and running my hands over him to make sure he was real. His feathers were soggy and cold and he was dripping sea water all over me, but I didn't care a bit. "I can't believe it's really you! Why did you leave? And where have you been all this time?"

I'd never wished for my pet duck to speak more than I did at that moment. Those questions had been

spinning around my brain for two whole days and I was dying to hear the answers. Would I ever know?

I pulled back a bit to get a good look at him. My eyes skimmed over his body. I was thrilled to discover that he looked just the same as always, except his white feathers were dirtier. And his satin bow tie had turned more of a muddy pink. He smelled a whole lot stinkier too. Maybe because he wasn't wearing a diaper anymore. From across the water, I could hear a chorus of quacking from the other ducks.

I crouched down so my face was eye-level with his. "Are you okay?"

He leaned his cheek against mine and clucked twice. My heart skittered with joy. That meant yes.

Or *si* in Italian.

Behind us, the quacking seemed to be getting louder. It sounded like those other ducks were having a conversation. Was this their way of saying goodbye to Webster?

"Let's go. Mombo will be so excited to see you!" I said, putting him down for a second so I could stand up. "Are you ready to come home now, baby?"

I clapped the sand off my hands and bent to pick him up again. He took a couple of waddling steps.

Backwards.

As in, away.

From me.

My stomach twisted into a painful knot. I held out my hands. "W-Webster?"

He cocked his head to the side and blinked up at me in that cute way he does when he wants something. But he didn't move.

Deep breaths.

"Waddle-Bunny?"

With a ruffle of feathers, he let out a single, soft quack. Then he turned and walked back into the water, his tufted white tail swinging adorably and a thin line of duck poop trailing behind him. My heart dropped into the sand as I watched him paddle across the cove toward the other ducks. He didn't even look back.

I stared after him in stunned silence. After all these years of me urging him to be more social, he'd finally made some friends of his own species.

Kinda like me, I guess.

I couldn't move. I was so sure he'd turn around and come back if I just waited long enough.

Webster swam up to one of the other ducks. A girl duck. I could tell by the colour of her feathers. He craned his neck and gave her a gentle cheek peck before darting ahead across the water. She caught up with him and gave him a peck back, then she darted away. And then they pressed repeat and did the whole routine all over again. Slowly it dawned on me.

Was Webster falling in love?

It felt like my stomach was being pulled inside out.

That darned bow tie! I knew it made him too handsome to resist!

JD came over and stood beside me. He didn't say anything, but his fingertips reached for mine and they felt warm and nice, so I didn't pull away when the rest of his hand wrapped around the rest of mine.

We watched Webster and his girlfriend swim and peck and cross over to the far bank and disappear into a thicket of reeds. Was there a nest in there? Was that Webster's new home?

I cupped a hand over my eyes to hide the tears I couldn't hold back anymore. I felt something go snap inside my chest.

Can your heart actually break in two?

Holy crumb, did it hurt.

JD dropped my hand and turned to face me. His mouth kept opening and closing, like he was struggling for the right words.

"I know this is hard, Mac," he said after a minute. "But it's still good, right? Webster's safe. And happy."

I could barely see him through my tears. "How can you *hic* say that? Nothing is ever good without him. If he doesn't come home with me, nothing is ever *hic* going to be good in my life again!"

How could it? Without my best friend by my side?

"He's with other ducks, Mac. Maybe this is what he wants."

I dragged a hand over my wet cheeks and sniffled back a fresh crop of tears. "But he's s-supposed to *hic* be with me!"

He couldn't possibly prefer his duck friends to his human mom. Right?

Could he?

Considering how upset I was, I thought JD might try a bit harder to comfort me. But he was weirdly silent. Then out of nowhere he flipped out, jumping back and thumping his chest like King Kong gone wild.

"Okay, fine!" he cried, grabbing the hem of his shirt like he was about to rip it off. "Do you want me to swim in after him, wrestle him away from his friends, drag him home, and lock him in a cage for you? 'Cause I'll do it!"

I stopped crying. My jaw fell open in surprise. Was he out of his freckle-covered mind? "What? No, of course not!"

He punched his fists to his hips, superhero-style, and raised his chin to the sky. "Are you sure? They don't call me Danger for nothing."

It took me a second to get it. Then my hands flew up to cover my face as a very vulgar snort exploded out of my nose. "You're a goofball," I giggled, giving him a slow clap. "That was supremely dramatic, though."

He uncurled his hands, dropped his chin, and morphed right back into himself. "Thanks," he said with a small bow. "Did I mention how I played Superman in our sixth-grade class play?"

"Why am I not surprised?" I replied, wiping the last of my tears away. I couldn't tell if these ones were from crying or laughing. "Does this mean I officially have permission to call you Danger now?"

"You better not," he said, suddenly serious. "Listen, Mac. I don't think there's anything more you can do for Webster right now. But there is someone else who needs us today."

"Who? It's not Madz, is it?"

"No. I'll tell you about it on the way to camp." He held out his hand again. "Let's go."

I glanced back to the spot in the reeds where Webster had disappeared. "But, I . . . he might . . ."

"Now that we know where he is, we can come back

and check on him again later today. Promise."

I nodded and swallowed hard.

His palm was still open, waiting for me to take it. "It's Ella, by the way," I added after a moment.

"What is?"

"My middle name." I shrugged. "I promised to tell you. So . . ."

JD smiled. "That's a whole lot nicer than Macaroni," he said, his eyes dropping to my necklace. "So is that the real reason you collect elephants?"

"No, I already told you why I collect them."

I was about to repeat my usual answer — about how elephants bring good luck. But a vague memory from a long time ago twitched in my brain. I wasn't sure I was remembering it clearly. Or if it was something I wanted to share.

Luckily, JD didn't have time for nosy questions. "Oof, it's getting late," he said, checking the time on his phone. "We better get moving." He waggled his hand to hurry me up.

I took one final glance back at the spot where Webster had disappeared into the reeds. For a split second, I thought about running in there after him. But then what? Drag him home and lock him in a cage? Like JD joked about?

195

"Love you, Feather Butt," I said softly. "I'll be back soon." Then I stepped forward and took JD's hand.

Deep breaths. "Okay, then . . ." I said. ". . . *Andiamo*."

Sandcastles in the Spot

By the time we left Webster's cove, the whole town seemed to have heard the news about the new beach. The tiny waterfront was so thick with gawking people, it made me wonder if maybe our population wasn't quite as rinky-dink as I'd once thought. I couldn't find Mombo in the crowd, so JD and I took a quick detour back to my apartment so I could check there. I couldn't wait to tell her about finding Webster! Our apartment was empty, but when I dug my phone out from under my bed, there was a whole whack of texts waiting for me. Including three from Mombo.

Had to leave. Couldn't find you and was late for work.
Wanna go back later and build a sandcastle?
See you at the big lunch!

I ran to the kitchen to show the messages to JD, who was busily looking through our fridge. "Shoot!" I said, "I forgot to tell my mother that the camp lunch is going to be cancelled."

He shut the fridge door with a *whump*, glanced at my phone, and smiled. "No worries, Mac. It's not cancelled. That's actually where we're heading now. Hey, can we borrow this for the day?" He held up a half-empty bottle of maple syrup.

"Sure. Wait . . . what?" I grabbed the syrup out of his hands. "Why isn't it cancelled? We don't know how to cook anything good. Let alone anything French. How the crust are we going to make a French feast for thirteen people?"

I was amazed he was even suggesting it. Gigi was right, it was doomed to be a huge disaster. And I, for one, didn't want to be humiliated in front of our families. I could almost imagine the lecture I'd get from Gran about how rude it was to drag her out of her house and force her to eat tasteless burnt food. And when she was done with me, she'd somehow figure out a way to blame Mombo for it all. Grandad would probably force himself to finish his plate of terrible food while trying to cover up his disappointment. Which was even worse because I'd still see it in his eyes.

"We have to cancel," I said, tossing the syrup down onto the counter. "Now. Before it's too late."

JD didn't want to hear it. "Trust me, it's all under control." He plucked the syrup up again and strode out of the kitchen. "But first we have to stop at the market to meet Madz. By the way, I just texted her the news about Webster. She's so happy, I think she's actually morphing into a smiley emoji."

That was a disturbing visual.

"I don't get it," I said, trailing after him. "Did you two learn the whole recipe book in the one day I was gone? Because I didn't cook a single edible thing this week."

"Not exactly. But we did manage to come up with a plan to turn it around. And save Gigi's job."

He reached for the door handle. I darted in front of him and blocked his way. "Why do you care so much about her job?" I demanded, crossing my arms in front of my chest. "She hasn't exactly been the nicest to us. Or Webster."

He smiled and curled his outstretched hand into a fist. "I have five good reasons," he said, popping his thumb. "One: I don't like the idea of having my name attached to a failing endeavour."

I sighed. JD was way too competitive for his own good.

"Two," he continued, sticking out his first finger. "As my father always says, two wrongs don't make a right."

I held up a hand to stop him right there. "Okay, true, but—"

"Three," he went on, adding another finger. "I insist on finishing this camp and earning my culinary arts certificate."

I rolled my eyes at that one. "Do you really think anyone's going to hire—"

"Four: What else are we going to do today?"

I lowered my hand. My thoughts skipped back to Webster and his new girlfriend. "We could go back and—"

He narrowed his eyes like he was reading my mind. "No, we can't. Because, five . . ." He paused with his freckled pinky in the air and waggled his eyebrows at me. "Gigi's been keeping a secret. And she needs our help."

Gigi's Secret

JD spilled the tea on our walk to the market. As it turns out, Madz was actually on to something with her wild conspiracy theories. No, not the ridiculous cut-and-pasted-cloud thing. Or the moon projection thing. The other one — the one about Chef Gigi.

And of course, the one day I was away from camp was the day all her messed-up dirty laundry came tumbling out.

"Right after you left with your mother yesterday morning, she broke down and told us everything," JD explained. "About how she's been straight-up lying to us all week."

"Us?"

"You, me, Madz, Mr. Cameron and the whole community centre staff. It's all a big sham."

"A sham? How?" I clutched my forehead. "I'm so rattled right now."

"Well, for starters, she's from Paris, Ontario . . . not Paris, France. And she's totally been faking that accent. Her name is Gina White, not Giselle LeBlanc. And she's not a superstar chef. Like at all. She's never even been to cooking school."

"Whaaaat?" I stopped walking. I was so stunned, my feet were going into shock. "Holy crumb!"

"Wait, it gets worse," JD said, pulling on my elbow. "But you have to move faster. We don't have much time."

"Okay," I said, letting him drag me forward. "Just keep talking."

"So, it turns out she flunked out of teachers' college last spring because of low attendance. Get this . . . instead of going to class, she was spending her days sitting at home watching the twenty-four hour cooking channel. Her parents freaked out and told her she had to get a job and pay them back the tuition money they'd loaned her. So when she saw this job, she applied for it. She'd seen so many cooking shows and figured she could fake her way through it. She also thought she'd have a better chance of landing a job out of town, where nobody knew who she was."

I couldn't believe what I was hearing. This was like something out of a book!

"But since she didn't have any credentials, she had to get creative." JD shot me a look. "You see why it's so important to start building your resumé early?"

For once, I couldn't bring myself to argue with him.

"She thought everyone would be impressed with a famous French chef, so she printed up some basic recipes from the internet. And she made up a whole new personality, complete with a phony accent and a snobby attitude. Can you believe it?"

Not really. I shook my head. "Did she have to make her new personality so mean?"

JD shrugged. "She said something about being inspired by a snooty French waiter in an old movie."

I rolled that around in my head for a second. If she wasn't from France, or snobby, or even a chef . . . who was she? "I'm shook. Why didn't we see through her act?"

"Nobody did. Except Madz. She was on to her this whole time."

I visored my eyes and peered up at the clouds, making a mental note to apologize for calling her theories ridiculous.

"So anyway," JD continued, "Gigi's big act all fell apart this week. For starters, she had no idea how to teach us how to cook and the community centre people started getting suspicious. Then her boyfriend found out about her lies and broke up with her, which shook her up pretty bad. She's an emotional wreck. And she's convinced herself that Mr. Cameron is coming to fire her today and her reputation will be ruined and she'll never work again."

"But doesn't she deserve it? Isn't all of this her own fault?"

"Yeah, I guess." He shrugged. "But I still feel kind of sorry for her. Here she is, alone in a strange town, in over her head at a job she lied to get. I don't think she's a bad person. She just made some really dumb choices."

We turned the corner onto Main Street. The food market was half a block away. "So, what's your big plan to help her?"

"Well, to start with, we're going to cook a French feast today."

"Really?" I pointed to my wrist. "Then I guess it's a good thing I'm wearing my lucky elephant bracelet. We're going to need all the help we can get."

JD sprang ahead of me and held open the market door. "Then as soon as I get my cooking certificate, I'm going to hook Gigi up with my agent," he added. "I think she's a natural-born actor."

Café 113

Madz was filling a shopping cart with bagged lettuce when we found her in the produce aisle. She was so excited to see me, she vaulted over a crate of oranges and threw her arms around me in a giant bear hug. "I knew we'd find Webster!" she yelled, squeezing me so hard, I thought I might snap. "I'm so freaking happy!"

"Hey . . . okay . . . ow!" I said, wrestling myself out of her grip.

"Ha. Sorry, not sorry," she grinned, punching my arm affectionately. The girl was dangerous when she was happy. Any more good news and I was going to end up bruised from head to toe. Her black T-shirt of the day read *Fluent in Sarcasm*.

We paid with the cash reward we didn't need for Webster anymore. The three of us arrived in room 113 just after nine o'clock, with heaping bags of groceries in our arms. Now that the heat wave had finally passed, the building was nice and cool again. Gigi was already there, slumped in a puddle over her desk. She looked up. A sad, wobbly frown tugged at her pale lips.

"Have you three come to watch me get fired?" she asked, her voice cracking slightly on that last word.

I was so surprised to hear her speaking without a "French" accent, I almost dropped my groceries.

"Nope," Madz said, tossing a large manila envelope onto the desk. "Have a look. We've come to cook a feast."

Gigi lifted her head and stared at the envelope.

"What's this?"

"Just open it, dude!"

Sitting up, Gigi lifted the flap and pulled out the top sheet of paper. She blinked hard as her gaze swept over the words. "You made menus?"

Madz dusted the pigtails off her shoulders. "Designed 'em myself."

"We've talked it over and we've come up with a way to help you out," JD said. "It's not going to be fancy. Or probably anywhere close to authentic. But I think we can pull this off."

A slow smile crept across Gigi's lips. Her gaze skipped over our faces. "Thank you," she whispered, her eyes bright with . . . whoa. Was she actually about to cry? I was already way too emotionally wrecked over what happened with Webster this morning. No way I could handle any more drama.

"All right. Let's get cooking!" I yelped, heaving my groceries onto the counter. The bag was so full, it tipped and a tall bottle of French salad dressing escaped from the top. It rolled quickly toward the edge. Luckily, Grandad's baseball training kicked in. I made a last-second dive and caught it before it crashed to the floor.

Madz and JD hooted and applauded in appreciation. "Great save, Mac!"

I giggled and took a quick bow.

Not exactly the outfield, but still pretty impressive.

Chef JD * Chef Madz * Chef Sarah
welcome you to a French feast
chez Café 113

-Hors d'oeuvres-
Frites with tomato confit
-Entrée du jour-
Salade verte
with sauce française
-Le dessert-
Pain doré à la mode
with drizzle d'érable
Bon appétit!

Lunch Is Served

As it turned out, cooking a French feast wasn't nearly as hard as I'd imagined. The three of us put together a pretty impressive meal, if I do say so myself.

The only thing we had to use the oven for were the french fries, and luckily we only burnt the first batch. The rest of them came out crispy, which is how I like them anyway. Madz swore it wasn't cheating, even though they came ready-to-bake, factory-made and frozen in a bag. "We're putting them on a pan and heating them in the oven all by ourselves, right?" she said. "Sorry, but in my family that totally counts as cooking!"

Our *Salade française* was pre-packaged lettuce tossed with French dressing. And our *Pain doré à la mode* with drizzle *d'érable*? That was French toast with French vanilla ice cream and maple syrup. It was the hardest dish to make. But Gigi helped us with the stove and the flipping and the presentation and it turned out absolutely edible. Maybe even kind of delicious.

We even had enough time left over to set the table! #Easypeasylemonsqueezy

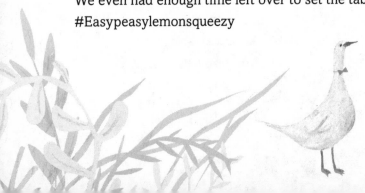

Our guests arrived promptly at noon. There was Mrs. Granger and Carly, Mombo, Gran and Grandad, Madz's parents and her little brother, Ethan. And Cousin Jerry, of course. But I think he was there more in an official capacity than as a guest.

Madz performed an interpretive tap dance solo to a dramatic monologue recited by JD while I plated the dishes and served. It was *très* theatric. I guess Gigi was right about one thing. We did end up putting on a show after all.

"Just don't tell my agent I performed for free," JD whispered as we sat down to eat. I had no idea who his agent was, but I promised anyway.

Madz was hoping the performances would be a good distraction from the food, in case it was terrible. We were all pretty nervous about how it was going to taste. I kept a close eye on our guests' plates and faces, and was relieved to see that most of them were empty. The plates, that is. Our families were laughing and talking with each other throughout the meal. Carly seemed to be having fun bossing Ethan around, making him fetch her extra napkins and more water. And Gran and Mrs. Granger were chatting up a storm.

See? I knew they'd get along!

Grandad sat next to Cousin Jerry and they spent

the entire meal discussing the new beach and debating the weather conditions that likely brought it back. And Mombo? She was sitting next to Gigi, and every time I looked over, they appeared to be having an intense discussion. But about what? Not me, I hoped. I was dying to know for sure. *Le dessert* was almost over and our guests would be leaving any minute. I was about to go over and insert myself into their conversation when there was a tap on my shoulder.

"Psst. Hey, Mac?" JD hissed from behind me.

I swung around in my seat. "Yeah?"

"Can you *pasta* maple syrup?" He snorted twice, then erupted into a laughing fit.

This time, I laughed with him.

After the four of us finished clearing the table, Madz went to her backpack and pulled out a pile of black T-shirts. "I know we don't technically need these any-more, since Webster's been found and all, but I think they're still nice souvenirs." She handed one each to me and JD. She even had one for Gigi. I held it up. Webster's sweet face stared back at me.

My vision went blurry. "Thank you," I croaked.

"My dudes!" she shrieked, throwing her arms around us. "This was by far the best week of my entire summer."

JD turned his head my way. His chocolate brown eyes seemed to melt into mine. "Me too," he agreed.

After everything that had happened with Webster, I couldn't say it was anything close to the best week. But it was definitely one I'd remember. Forever.

"I think the three of us make a pretty good team," I said, squeezing them so tight, I didn't know how I was ever going to let go. I can't believe I was so sad to be finished with cooking camp. Five days ago, I could never have imagined this moment was possible.

"Totally," JD said. "We crushed it in the kitchen today!"

When Madz finally released us from her grip, her face was the same shade of red as her pigtails. "Maybe we could, like, hang out when school starts next week?" she asked, scuffing a smudge on the floor with the toe of her army boot.

"For sure," I said, holding up my hand for a high-five.

"And hey, maybe next summer we can all try out that wilderness camp together?" JD added. "That kind of thing looks great on a resumé."

Before heading back to the beach house (which was suddenly no longer a misnomer), Gran and Grandad came over to say goodbye.

"Great work today, Sarah!" Grandad said, pulling me into a hug. It was good to see him up and out of that chair again. "Maybe you'll teach us some of your recipes?"

"Anytime."

Gran stood on tiptoe to kiss my cheek. "Congratulations, Sarah dear. It was a very successful luncheon."

"Thanks. I was actually thinking about your advice the whole time."

"Really?" Her pencilled eyebrows shot up in surprise. "What advice was that?"

"You told me it's always right to make people feel welcome. And it's always right to feed them. And that people appreciate kindness."

"Well, I'm glad somebody around here listens to me." Her eyes flicked over to Grandad. I saw him give her a smile and a little nod. "You should know that I've decided to take your advice too."

I stared at her in surprise. "My advice?"

"Yes. About my friend's painting." She paused to pick an imaginary stray hair off her sleeve. "You were right, it had no business gathering dust under my bed."

"Are you serious?" I couldn't believe what I was hearing. My Gran never agreed with anyone. What was going on?

"I never joke about art," she said sternly. "After you and your mother left on Wednesday night, I decided to take the painting out and hang it up for your grandfather. Just as you suggested. Except now that the beach has come back, he insists he doesn't want it hanging there and distracting him from his view. And it really didn't fit with the other art in the house. And I couldn't be bothered to tape it back up in all that dusty bubble wrap. So . . . it's yours. Do with it as you wish. Hang it up. Or tuck it under your own bed. Or sell it and travel around the world." She paused for a second here. Was she holding back a smile? "Do whatever you like."

Was this for real? I glanced at Grandad, hoping for an explanation. He shot me a quick wink.

"But . . . but you said it was priceless."

"Pshaw!" Gran said, with a flick of her hand. "It was given to me as a gift. And so now I'm gifting it to you. Think of it as a late birthday present. Now, dear . . ." Her voice dropped down to a whisper, "I must warn you that there's quite a bit of lettuce stuck in your teeth. You might want to go brush it out. It's terribly vulgar."

I was too shocked about the painting to bother explaining about my new elastics. This was quickly turning out to be the strangest day of my life. By a landslide. And it was only lunchtime.

After he'd finished handing out our certificates, Cousin Jerry shook Gigi's hand.

"Nicely executed, Miss LeBlanc. I'm glad it all came together in the end. Perhaps you'd consider coming back and running cooking camp for another session next year?"

Gigi flashed him her biggest, brightest smile. And I wondered if maybe that was the one thing that hadn't been part of her act.

"Perhaps," she replied mysteriously.

Deleted

That evening, Mombo and I went back to the beach so I could show her Webster's cove. I'd told her about his new home, but she wanted to see it for herself. At some point during the day, his bow tie must have fallen off. And since he didn't wear a diaper anymore, he looked ridiculously naked. Although I guess to anyone else he probably looked like a regular duck. But it didn't make much of a difference to me either way. I'm his mom. I'd recognize him anywhere, with or without his accessories.

I had some birdseed with me, and maybe he smelled it because he came charging straight out of the water and immediately started pecking at my pockets. Was he hungry? Did he know where to find food on his own out here? He'd never had to live in the wild before. Were the other ducks teaching him how to survive? Gosh, I hoped so.

"How nice to see you again, Webster," Mombo said, stroking his feathers. "You look wonderful."

It broke my heart to admit that she was right. He was dripping wet and smudged with dirt and he had a gleam in his eyes and a extra bounce to his step and he reminded me of a little kid who'd been having the time of his life playing unsupervised in a mud puddle. He'd clearly been having fun these past two days. What if this was the life he was actually meant to be living? Like, maybe he should always have been splashing it up in a pond instead of living in an apartment.

And then a question flashed through my mind — a question so horriblicious it sent my heart dropping into my stomach. Have I been holding him back all these years? Have I been keeping him from discovering true duck happiness?

I blinked hard, trying my best to erase that question and think of something else. Fast.

"So, ah . . . what were you and Gigi talking about at lunch?" I asked, combing a small leaf out of Webster's feathers with one hand as he nibbled a seed out of the other.

"Oh, you know . . ." Mombo flicked her hand casually. "Cooking stuff. And the hard year she's had. I think she really needed someone to talk to."

"Did you hear Jerry asked her to come back and teach the camp again next year?"

"I wouldn't bet on that happening." Mombo sang in that frustrating I-know-a-secret way of hers.

"Why not?"

"I really shouldn't say, but . . ." She smiled and gestured for me to come closer. "Just between you and me?"

"Always!" I said, leaning in. This sounded good. I didn't want to miss a word.

"I offered her an internship at our catering shop. And she accepted. Isn't that great?" Mombo's blue eyes were wide with excitement. "We really need an extra pair of hands and Gigi — sorry, *Gina* — needs some legitimate culinary experience. It felt meant to be. I told her if she was serious about becoming a proper chef, this was a good first step."

"So, wait. She's moving to the Spot?" I couldn't believe what I was hearing. Mombo and Gigi were going to be working together? "Like, permanently?"

"I don't know about permanently. But at least for the next little while. Apparently, she's not in any kind of hurry to go back to Paris."

Paris, Ontario or Paris, France? I had to wonder how much of the truth she'd confessed to Mombo at lunch today. Did she use her French accent? Or her real one? I was bursting with questions.

But before I could ask any of them, Webster finished his snack and turned to head back toward the water. I stood up to wave goodbye as he shook out his feathers and waddled across the beach.

I flumped back down into the sand. There was a part of me that had been hoping he'd still want to come home with us, now that he'd had two full days of adventure. Mombo and I sat there for a long time, watching him paddle around with his new duck friends. I waited for her to say something wise and comforting and expertly motherish. She didn't. So I didn't say anything either. But she must have heard me sad-sniffling because after a few minutes, her arm wrapped around my shoulders.

"Remember that time Webster thought the plastic rubber ducky in our bathtub was real? And he kept poking it with his beak and trying to get it to play with him?"

"Yeah, of course," I said, wiping my nose. "Remember how much he used to love blowing bubbles in the bath water?"

Mombo laughed. "I think we even have a video of that somewhere."

"And remember how every Easter he used to sit on my basket of chocolate eggs for hours, like he thought maybe they'd hatch?" I smiled at the memory. "H-he was always such a thoughtful d-duck . . ." Now my throat was closing up. I turned my face into her shoulder and let out a sob.

"It doesn't mean he doesn't love you," she said, squishing me close. "But you can't hold someone back if they're determined to fly away."

She was looking right at Webster when she said that. But I think we both knew she was talking about Papa too.

"Pekin ducks can't fly," I croaked, glancing up at her from under my lashes. Her eyebrows were doing that twitchy, jerky thing and I heard her pull in a long, shaky breath. My stomach muscles tightened, like they were getting ready for a punch.

"The last I heard from your father was nine years ago. He'd been away six months when I got the letter. He'd written it from an ashram somewhere in the mountains of Northern India. He didn't say much more. Just that he was sorry he couldn't be the father and husband we deserved."

I tucked that bit of information away inside my heart.

"Did he say goodbye?" I asked after a minute. "Like, officially. In the letter?"

Her other hand reached for mine. "No."

I nodded. "What's an ashram?"

"A place of spiritual retreat."

"Is he still there?"

She shook her head. "I really couldn't say for sure, but I doubt it. Your Gran used to say that your father was like a shark. Fearless, solitary, restless. He had to keep moving or he'd die."

I thought about the collection of travel posters hanging on my wall. At least two of them were from cities in India. It was hard to imagine that Papa might have been there all this time. And then a thought occurred to me: *Was I like a shark too? Was that another bit of DNA we shared? Like our curly hair?*

"Gran also used to say that *I* was more like an elephant," Mombo continued. "Steady. Strong. Practical. Loyal . . ." Her voice trailed off.

My ultra-dainty mother, like an elephant? A memory twitched in my brain. Something Madz said this week. *"Female elephants rear the children. They feed and protect the herd. They support each other. Those girls do it all."*

"Yeah, I can see that. I think I even remember Gran saying it."

"Do you?" Mombo squeezed my hand. "Yes, she's always been generous with her opinions. Before we got married, she took me aside and told me that it was dangerous for sharks and elephants to live together. She said a tragic outcome was inevitable — someone would end up either drowned or trampled." She let out a sad laugh. "I ignored her advice at the time. But I have to admit that she was right."

I took a few minutes to consider that. Pretty sure I knew which one of them drowned and which one got trampled.

"I deleted that FindYourPeeps app on my phone," I said, resting my head on her shoulder. "I'm so sorry I went behind your back. I never wanted to hurt your—"

"Shush, now," she said, cutting me off. "*I'm* the one who should apologize. I'm sorry I made you feel like a criminal for wanting to know more about your father. I suppose I've just been scared."

"Of what?"

"Of everything," she replied gently. "That I might lose you. That your father might show up and try to take you from me. Or that you'll just up and leave me one day. Like he did. And I just couldn't imagine my life without you." I couldn't see her face, but I knew by the hitches in her voice that she was crying now too.

"I suppose that's why I'm so overprotective," she continued. "And why I stopped talking about him with you. Remember how we used to look for him in the big world atlas together? I swear, I could see him right there in your eyes every time we'd open it up. You'd get that same look . . . like you wanted to reach out and grab the world with both hands. You were so eager and you asked so many questions, it terrified me. I hid that atlas away on the highest shelf in the house. I guess I thought hiding it away would somehow keep you from following in his footsteps. I was so wrong."

My hand fluttered up to my elephant necklace. I clasped it tight. "Mombo . . ."

"You are the person you're meant to be. I should never have tried to crush your wandering spirit." Then she laughed. Definitely more of a tragic kind of laugh than funny-ha-ha. "I should have known I was in trouble when you asked for a passport on your eighth birthday." By now, I was so teary I was in danger of melting into a puddle of salt water. I had to mop my eyes with the hem of my T-shirt just so I could see.

"I might look like him, but I'm *not* Papa. Just because I want to see the world one day, doesn't mean I'm going to leave you behind." I paused, then added, "Maybe, you could even come with me?"

"You don't know how much I would love that." She turned slightly and planted a kiss on the top of my curls. "Darling. If you want to search for him, I won't stand in your way anymore."

I shook my head. "Maybe one day he'll decide he

wants to come back and see me. He knows where I am. But if not, that's okay too."

"You didn't have to delete the app."

"Yeah, I did. I don't want to find out about my father that way." I took a deep breath, sat up straight, and turned to face her. Mombo's cheeks were just as drenched as mine. "I'd rather find out about him from you."

She reached out to wipe a stray tear off the tip of my nose. Her hand was trembling.

"All right. What do you want to know?"

I swallowed hard. "How about everything?"

"Oh my!" She laughed nervously. "That could take a while." She clapped the sand off her hands and rose to her feet. "It's starting to get dark. Let's go home and talk about it over some marshmallow smoothies."

We linked arms as we made our way up the sand toward the lighthouse. But a moment later, there was an eruption of noise from behind.

I spun around to see Webster waddling up the beach toward us. He was honking loudly and flapping his wings so hard, for a second I thought he might actually take flight. In the distance, I could see his two duck friends paddling in small circles around the cove.

Mombo stopped walking and frowned.

"What's wrong with Webster?"

"Maybe he's still hungry?" I stepped forward as he approached and held up my empty hands. "Sorry, buddy, I'm all out of birdseed." He squawked and shook out his feathers, sprinkling my bare toes with a shower of tiny, cool drops. "Don't worry. I'll bring more food tomorrow." I glanced over to where his friends were swimming. "I'll bring some for them too. Okay?"

He let out a sigh, cocked his head to the side, and stared silently up at me. His white feathers glowed brightly against the evening sky. I could tell he was waiting for something.

"What is it?" I asked, suddenly concerned. I knelt down into the sand beside him and looked into his eyes. "Don't you want to be with your friends?"

He shuffled forward and nipped at the sleeve of my T-shirt. A low groan escaped from his beak. Clearly, he was trying to tell me something.

"What do you suppose he wants?" Mombo asked.

"I'm not sure."

By now Webster was clucking loudly and tugging so hard at my sleeve, I thought he might rip it off. He'd never done this before. What did it mean? I leaned closer and studied his sweet little face. Was he . . . was he trying to ask me to stay? He'd always been so hyper-aware of my feelings. He was probably sensing my sadness.

Of course. That must be it.

My baby was worried about me.

"You're such a good friend," I said, stroking his head as I blinked back a fresh crop of hot tears. More than anything, I wanted to scoop him up into my arms and carry him home and never let him out of my sight again. But was that what he'd want? Wasn't this cove his home now?

"Sarah, darling?" Mombo said, squatting down beside us. "Is he okay?"

"I'm not sure." My thoughts skipped back to something she'd said earlier. About me. And her. I let out a shaky breath.

I desperately wanted Webster to come home. But I didn't want to stop him if he was ready to discover the world. I loved him way too much to ever crush his wandering spirit.

Lifting my chin, I forced out a smile. I could only hope it looked convincing. "Don't worry about me, Feather Butt," I said lightly. "I'm going to be just fine. Your job is done. It's time for you to live your own life now. And for me to live mine." I nodded toward the cove. "Go on."

He didn't move. In fact, if I didn't know better,

I'd think he was actually digging his feet even deeper into the sand than before. I wrestled what was left of my sleeve out of his beak, lifted him up and turned him back in the direction of the water. My vision was so blurry with tears, I could barely see straight. "Go! Now!" I grunted, rocketing to my feet and charging up the beach.

"Darling, wait!" Mombo called after me. But I couldn't wait. I had to keep moving. Before I changed my mind. A second later, I froze in my tracks as a long, wailing honk fell over my ears. Echoing across the water, it was the most hauntingly, heart-breakingly lonely sound I'd ever heard in my life. It lasted for about ten seconds, then stopped abruptly. I turned around and peered through the fading light. Webster was standing there, all naked and muddy and looking so small and alone on that wide expanse of beach. Even from a distance, I could see his little feathered chest rising and falling so fast. Too fast.

He was panting again.

Duck distress.

Only this time, it had nothing to do with the weather. And everything to do with me.

"Go to him, Sarah," Mombo said." He needs you."

In that second, it hit like a lightning bolt to the brain

– it's not *me* he's worried about this time. It's himself. As much fun as he's had on his adventure, he can't live without us.

Without *me*.

I ran toward him, my arms open wide like a pair of wings.

I was Webster's emotional support person. No way I was ever going to let him down.

Seven Things I Found Out about Papa

1. Everyone in the Spot called him Nick.

But Mombo called him Nicco. And he called her Cara. Short for Caroline. It's also Italian for *dear*. Adorable, right? They really did love each other once.

2. His favourite food to cook was spaghetti with bolognese sauce.

His mother's recipe. It was also his favourite food to eat.

3. He played the ukulele.

And he had a good singing voice. Mombo said he used to serenade me to sleep with Italian lullabies.

4. He was charming.

And he had an infectious laugh. Mombo said "to know him was to love him."

5. He liked country music, old movies and big, slobbery dogs.

6. It wasn't my fault that he left.

7. Most likely, he's not coming back.

Paddling Furiously

We head down to Webster's cove every morning to visit his duck friends. Even when it rains. I always bring a pocketful of treats for them. I know they look forward to our visits because they start quacking and waddling up the beach as soon as they see us. And I love it. My heart feels like it's going to burst open with happiness every time.

I know they aren't technically my pets, but I decided to name the other two ducks Rocky and Sandy. Those felt like good names. Rocky's favourite snack is corn. But Sandy likes birdseed best. Just like her boyfriend.

Even though Webster lives with me, it's obvious from the way they look at each other that they're still in love.

With Webster being a local celebrity, news about his return spread fast around the Spot. I got at least a dozen offers of puppies, gerbils, kittens and even a corn snake from concerned people who wanted me to have a back-up pet, just in case Webster ever decided to wander off again. But I didn't want to think about that possibility. And I didn't want another pet. My heart belongs to Webster forever.

A few weeks ago, Mrs. Granger and her BBTS Ladies' Auxiliary surprised me by unveiling an official *Webster's Cove* sign on the beach, along with a wooden bench where people could sit if they wanted to come relax and watch Rocky and Sandy paddling around. There's even a plaque on the side of it, explaining what sort of food is safe and not safe to feed them.

#howawesomeisthat?

The bench feels almost like a second home to us now. Sometimes Mombo comes to Webster's Cove with us. Sometimes JD and Madz meet us there. But usually it's just me and Webster. It's a good place to sit quietly, watch the ducks swim and the breeze blow over the water, write in my notebook and sink into some deep thoughts.

I spend a lot of time thinking about what Grandad said that day Webster first went missing. How if you spend too much time dwelling on the things you've lost, you might not notice what you've got in its place. And how sometimes those things can be just as wonderful. But in a different way.

Did I mention that my Grandad is the best?

And then I think about how some people in life come

and go, while others stay with you for the long haul. And how you can't ever control any of it.

All you can do is love them while they're here.

I'm probably never going to figure out how to be calm on the surface, like a duck. And I don't like the idea of being solitary, like a shark.

I've decided I'd rather be strong, like an elephant. Like Mombo.

I don't think of us as abandoned or broken anymore. Because we're not. And we never have been.

We're elephants.

Our own perfect little herd of two.

How lucky is that?

I wonder why I never realized it before.

And then I wonder if I actually knew it all along.

Dear Papa,

This is my last letter to you. I know you won't actually get it, but I'm writing the words anyway. Because I think it's important to say goodbye.

I'm sorry you decided not to be part of our lives. Mombo explained everything. I guess it's not your fault you were born a shark. It's just too bad for us.

In case you're ever wondering, I'm going to be okay. I hope you are too, wherever you are. I won't be searching for you anymore. If you ever want to see me, you know where to find me.

Only don't come looking for me in the Spot next summer. I'll be at wilderness camp with my friends in July. And on safari in August, hanging with the elephants.

Mombo and I just applied for our passports.

And Webster's excited to finally get a chance to fly . . .

Ciao,
Sarah